Between the Sea and Sky

ALSO BY JACLYN DOLAMORE

Magic Under Glass

Between the Sea and Sky

JACLYN DOLAMORE

BLOOMSBURY

NEW YORK BERLIN LONDON SYDNEY

First published in the United States of America in October 2011
by Bloomsbury Books for Young Readers
www.bloomsburyteens.com

For information about permission to reproduce selections from this book, write to
Permissions, Bloomsbury BFYR, 175 Fifth Avenue, New York, New York 10010

Library of Congress Cataloging-in-Publication Data
Dolamore, Jaclyn.
Between the sea and sky / by Jaclyn Dolamore. — 1st U.S. ed.
        p.   cm.
Summary: Esmerine, a mermaid, grows close to her childhood playmate Alander, a winged man,
when they join forces to find her sister Dosia, who has reportedly eloped with a human despite the
sisters' vow to always keep the sea and its people first in their hearts.
ISBN 978-1-59990-434-4
[1. Mermaids—Fiction. 2. Sisters—Fiction. 3. Love—Fiction.
4. Runaways—Fiction. 5. Magic—Fiction.] I. Title.
PZ7.D6975Bet 2011   [Fic]—dc22   2010038094

Book design by Regina Roff
Typeset by Westchester Book Composition
Printed in the U.S.A. by Quad/Graphics, Fairfield, Pennsylvania
2 4 6 8 10 9 7 5 3 1

To my parents, for giving me a lifetime of love and creative space

Between the Sea and Sky

Chapter One

It was not every day that a mermaid became a siren, and not every day that Esmerine attended such a party. It seemed just yesterday that she had moped at home while her older sister, Dosinia, had spent the week in a whirlwind of ceremony and celebration for her siren's debut. Now Esmerine's turn had come.

"Yes, this is Esmerine, my second to oldest." Esmerine's mother put her arm around her daughter for perhaps the fiftieth time that evening.

"Well!" The older merwoman, her neck laden with pearls, made a slight dip. "Congratulations, Mrs. Lornamend—"

"Lorre*men*," her mother corrected. Everyone knew of the Lornamend merchant family, but the Lorremens were fishermen, and their name was hardly on the lips of society. "You may remember that my eldest daughter, Dosinia, was granted a siren's belt two years ago."

"Oh, of *course*," the older woman said. "Miss Dosinia, yes. She's a lovely young woman."

"Esmerine here is the brain of the family," Esmerine's mother continued. "She has a wonderful head for remembering songs and histories."

Esmerine smiled dutifully. Dosinia—Dosia to her sisters—was the pretty one, while she was the brain, and if they ever forgot, their mother would surely remind them.

The old woman paused in thought, her rather short tail gently waving. "Wasn't it one of your daughters who used to play with that little winged boy?" She frowned at Esmerine a little, disapproving the behavior even before it was confirmed.

"Oh goodness, that was years ago! I had quite forgotten," her mother said, clearly a lie, for Esmerine was still teased about her friendship with Alander from time to time. She hadn't seen him in years, but the fact that she used to play with him— and worse, that he had taught her to read—had branded her as peculiar.

"I'm glad he doesn't come around anymore," the old woman continued. "Those people ought to keep a better eye on their children." She gave Esmerine's mother a pointed look, as if she should have done so herself.

"Excuse me," Esmerine said, catching Dosia's eye across the room. She swam upward with a flick of her tail.

Esmerine barely saw her sister these days. Even if Esmerine hadn't been busy preparing for her siren's initiation, Dosia was almost never home. Esmerine suspected she had a new beau.

Dosia stopped munching on olives long enough to wrap her arms around Esmerine's shoulders. "Finally!" Dosia squealed in her ear. They had been wishing all their lives to do something truly exciting together, and now that day had come. They would both be sirens.

Esmerine reached for an olive, glancing around for a server. "Where'd you get those?" she asked Dosia.

"They were just passing them out a minute ago. I'll share. They've got almonds inside." Dosia gave half her olives to Esmerine. Esmerine's mother only bought olives when good company was expected, complaining all the while about giving the traders a whole fish for a paltry handful of the surface-world treat.

"Don't tell me you're tired of trailing Mother around and meeting all those charming old rich ladies?" Dosia said with a grin.

"My favorite part," Esmerine said, "is that they keep calling us *Lornamends*."

Dosia groaned. "I remember the same thing from my initiation, and I think they only do it so we're forced to correct them. Well, it doesn't matter, the rest of the sirens are lovely. This is the only night you have to endure these old matrons." Dosia made a face as a gentleman mer brushed by, his numerous strands of shell jewelry almost catching in her hair.

"Let's go up near the ceiling until the ceremony," Esmerine said. "It's so crowded here." Most of the mers had gathered at the bottom of the room, clinging to sculpted rocks or clustering by the floating lanterns.

"I thoroughly agree." Dosia grabbed Esmerine's arm and swished her tail, drawing them both up along the gently tapering walls. She stopped at a rock that jutted out not far from where water-freshening bubbles from an underground air pocket flowed through an opening in the ceiling. Although the bubbles occasionally obscured the view below, they had the space to themselves.

"So where have you been these past couple of weeks?" Esmerine asked. "I've hardly seen you."

"You've just been busy," Dosia said. "I've been around."

Esmerine raised her brows. "Hardly. And I haven't seen much of Jarra either." Dosia was always coy when a boy first caught her interest, but it was no secret that she had favored Jarra at dances lately.

Dosia paused, looking back toward the bottom of the room, where the water churned with movement. "Jarra?" She shook her head. "I haven't seen him either."

"Well then, who?"

"Maybe I'm not interested in a *boy*," Dosia said. She looked embarrassed, which was odd for her.

The soft orbs of magic lights dimmed, signaling that the show would begin soon. The siren's ceremony would follow, and Esmerine knew she ought to take her place with Lady

Minnaray in preparation, but she preferred to watch with Dosia.

The lights snuffed. Esmerine could hardly see Dosia's face. The eerie sound of female voices rose from the seafloor. Three merwomen appeared, pushing a softly glowing rock as tall as their length into the center of the floor.

Additional magical lights floated down through the opening in the ceiling, briefly illuminating Dosia's face as they passed. Mermen with their tails formed into legs and dressed in tattered clothes kicked their way down from the skylight. Behind them followed pairs of mermen bearing white sails to represent the ship the humans rode.

The song of the women on the floor had faded, and now the men began to sing, mimicking the sea chanteys of human sailors. *If the winds hold fair we'll catch that whale, and if our luck is true, boys, we'll catch a mermaid too . . .*

As they sang, the rock on the floor cracked down the middle, releasing a narrow beam of light. The mermaid singers pried the rock open, revealing a mermaid nestled in a crystal lining, her rare red hair floating about her. Strands of tiny glowing beads ran through her hair, and a faux golden siren's belt glinted around her narrow waist.

O sisters, what handsome voice crept into my slumbering ear and brought to me a waking dream? The mermaid's pure, powerful voice put Esmerine's neighborhood singing club to shame.

One of the "human" men swam down, lured by her song. They locked eyes, and she began to drift toward him.

Sister, no! Come back! sang the mermaid chorus.

The other sirens pulled at her arms and fins, and she shook her head like she knew she'd been a fool, but in another moment she began to drift up again. The siren and the human man grew ever more enraptured by one another, until finally he slid her belt from her waist and she fainted dramatically into his arms, her tail splitting into legs with one final convulsion. The mermen bearing sails scattered around them while the sirens fled to a dark corner, cooing a sad song for the one they had lost. The merman actor did a magnificent job of portraying a human struggling to drag the mermaid's body to shore.

Dosia and Esmerine sighed at the romance and the tragedy to come. They knew this story well. Not a week went by when even the poorest merfolk didn't gather in homes and taverns to share songs and stories of their history.

As the next act began, the human man brought the siren to his home. Props brought from shipwrecks formed the stage set. She tried to please her new husband, but tongues of black "flame" from the seaweed fireplace burned her and she shied back from his horse—played by a muscular merman wearing a sea horse mask. Her husband finally lost patience, striking her across the face. The audience booed him with a passion.

"Humans aren't really like that," Dosia whispered.

"As if you've met one," Esmerine said. Dosia could be a real know-it-all about humans sometimes.

Dosia grinned. "I'd never be so stupid if I was a human's wife."

"I'd *love* to ride a horse," Esmerine said.

Dosia squeezed Esmerine's hand. "Me too."

In a final bid to win her husband's love, the siren confessed she was with child. His hand paused, midstrike, and suddenly he broke into a song of love, demonstrating his poor human values. Esmerine couldn't stand such moralistic tales, but of course the village elders hoped to scare the young sirens away from humans.

The lights dimmed as the stagehands cleared the props away. The somber opera of human cruelty and siren folly was followed by a trio of mermen who sang familiar comedic songs.

"We learned these in the nursery," Dosia scoffed.

"They can't get too bawdy, not with all these old ladies sponsoring it."

"Still, the Fish Song? They might as well not even bother."

One of the singing mermen noticed them talking and sang precisely in Dosia's direction, flourishing with an arm. Dosia huddled even closer to Esmerine.

"Oh *no*," she groaned.

"Don't even look at them anymore," said Esmerine.

"I won't. Anyway, you should probably find Lady Minnaray."

It was almost time for her siren's initiation. Esmerine hadn't allowed herself to think much of it, and her stomach had been in such a constant state of anxiety during the last few days that she had grown used to it. Being a siren was a great honor, an exalted place in mer society. No reason to be nervous, Lady Minnaray told her, but new initiates always were.

The possibilities of childhood—that she might grow up to be an actress or a human pirate or a fisherwoman—had always been a game and an illusion, Esmerine realized. Her world was here. Nonetheless, it was scary to think of reciting the siren's pledge in front of everyone she knew, and commit to one life forever.

She approached Lady Minnaray shyly. The eldest siren was tanned and wrinkled from a lifetime of sitting on the rocks, and she had a regal bearing despite her small size.

"You look lovely, Esmerine," Lady Minnaray said. "No need for such wide eyes."

"I'll be fine."

"I know you will."

Two of the other older sirens, Lady Minnaray's friends, gathered closer with reassuring words. "It's hard to believe it's already been three years since we chose you. You and Dosia must be so excited!"

Every year, the village schools put on a weeklong festival where the children sang and displayed magic for the village elders. If the sirens and elders saw potential in any of the children, they would pull them aside for further testing, and a few fortunate girls were chosen to train as sirens. They were given a belt of enchanted gold, the links thin but impossibly strong and impervious to corrosion. For the next few years, the young sirens would learn to infuse the belt with magic, to tap into the magic when needed, and to enhance its powers as the years went by. By harnessing the magic outside themselves, their power grew. They learned the finer details of siren song, the power of their voices. And they would be warned, time and time again, of the danger of human men.

The trio of merman singers finished, and Lady Minnaray moved toward center stage, gesturing for Esmerine to follow. The other older sirens took up the rear according to their rank. The audience was full of the faces of young sirens like Dosia, all smiling and welcoming. Esmerine clutched at her bead necklace, trying to stay calm.

"I present to you Esmerine Lorremen," Lady Minnaray said, her voice a song even when she spoke. "She has completed her training and is ready to take her place as a guardian of our waters."

An attendant brought out the ceremonial shell, as big as Esmerine's head, and opened it to reveal the golden belt Esmerine had spent so many hours filling with magic. Lady Minnaray lifted the belt by its clasps, and presented one end to Esmerine. For a moment, the belt was a chain between them.

Esmerine repeated her pledge after Lady Minnaray.

"*I promise to serve as a daughter of the sea. For as long as I live and it is within my power, I shall protect the sea and all its denizens from the human race, even if it means disregarding my own desires.*" Esmerine swallowed, remembering the day when the elder sirens explained how to wreck a fishing boat that took more than its share of fish and how to drown a human swiftly. She spoke the next words quickly; she wished to have them over with.

"*The water is my mother, my father, my first love, and sworn duty.*

Should I have children, I will keep my belt safe for them, for the safety and strength of my people. With the donning of this belt, I give myself to the sea and its people forevermore."

How often had those words been spoken and then ignored? Esmerine wondered as she lifted her dark-brown waist-length hair out of the way so Lady Minnaray could fasten the belt just below her navel.

"Now you are one of us," Lady Minnaray said.

Chapter Two

"Well, you're a true siren now, Esmerine," her father said proudly. Her parents and Dosia were waiting for her when she left the center of the great room. The crowd was already beginning to disperse and resume conversations. "How does it feel?"

"Good." Esmerine didn't know what else she could say. Maybe it was impossible to achieve a great honor without feeling numb.

"Two sirens in the family," her mother said. "I would never have guessed it. Not a single siren in our entire family history, and now two! You girls are truly treasures." Not only did sirens bring prestige to a family, but even after death, a siren's belt was passed down through generations and could be used in times of need to work powerful healing spells or even defend the village. The status of Esmerine's family would be forever elevated from mere fishermen.

When Esmerine, Dosia, and their parents arrived home, Esmerine's youngest sister, Merramyn, was swimming to and fro, adorning the cave walls with flower chains. Tormaline, usually the most serious of the sisters, was moving the magic lights to find the best position. Esmerine's mother swept in to interfere.

"Tormy, what are you doing? I said put one in the middle of the room and—wait, where is the fourth?"

"*Mother*, we don't have a fourth." Tormy was thirteen, and lately she had taken to saying "Mother" in a particularly irritated way.

"We should have four. This one is ours, and I rented three."

"You rented two. You decided to save the rest of the money to buy sea bass, remember?"

Merramyn twirled through the water, draping the last flower chain around her shoulders. Dosia tried to take it from her. "Merry, don't be silly with that, you're going to damage it."

A flower broke free from the garland and swished around Merry's hair. She snatched it. "Dosia, look! Now you broke it! Mother, Dosia broke the flowers!"

As Esmerine swam out of the main room, she made a silent prayer to the sea gods that her family would make it through the evening without embarrassing her. Through the narrow door to the kitchen, her poor aunts were preparing food for a crowd with only one magic light to see by. The cave was old and had few windows, just small holes to keep water flowing in and big fish out. In wealthier homes, window nets kept out the fish *and* let in light.

Fragments of seaweed drifted through the water from the salad Aunt Celwyn was making, while Aunt Lia tucked bits of neatly sliced raw fish into empty seashells for presentation.

"Can I help?" Esmerine asked.

"Chase out this silly fish that keeps bothering me." Aunt Lia waved her hand as a slender fish darted past her face and into the shadowy corners. Just as Esmerine chased the fish out with the net, Dosia hooted a summons from the main room.

"The guests must be arriving," Aunt Celwyn said. "Go on and greet them! This is your day."

Esmerine raked her fingers through her hair, checking that her beads were still in place before she returned to the main room for hugs and congratulations. The guests arrived in a steady stream: her mother's friends, the fishermen who worked along-side her father, friends she and Dosia had made in school and in their neighborhood singing group.

She knew the routine from when Dosia had become a siren, and although she blushed and said humble things, she was secretly pleased to have a little piece of the attention Dosia had gotten for so long.

At dinner, her aunts brought the food around. Esmerine wished they had servants, particularly since her mother had invited Lalia Tembel and her family. Esmerine and Lalia had been casual friends for years now, but Esmerine had never forgotten how Lalia had teased her about playing on the islands and for her lack of bracelets when they were little. Lalia also used to tell Esmerine that if she spent too much time in human form, she'd get stuck that way, and even when Esmerine had Dosia tell her off, Lalia had never apologized.

Still, her mother had not skimped on the food. They had the freshest fish, rare sea fruits sent from the Balla Sea, almonds and hazelnuts, enough olives that Esmerine had her fill for the first time in her life, and sea potatoes filled with minced shrimp.

They sang the Siren's Hymn in her honor, her mother's eyes growing red and wistful.

Come and hear the siren's call
Keep mankind in fearful thrall
As long as sirens guard the sea
All the waters shall be free!

Dosia, sitting beside Esmerine, squeezed her hand tight, and Esmerine knew she was thinking how wonderful it would be to be sirens together.

"Well, we ought to bring around the gifts, if anyone's going to sleep tonight!" her father finally said.

Esmerine received all the things she expected: necklaces of shell, a new brush and comb, the matched earrings and tail jewelry that had come into fashion lately—the last from the Tembels, of course, who wouldn't give anything less than fashionable even though Esmerine refused to pierce her tail fins and

Lalia knew it. Her parents gave her the most beautiful bright-red headdress of beads to wear in her hair, much like the blue one Dosia had.

"I have a present for you too," Dosia said.

"Oh? But I didn't give you a present when you became a siren . . ."

"That's all right, because I'm older. And I have just the thing. Tormy and Merry helped me hide it."

Merry giggled and hurried to her sleep room with a flick of her tail that disrupted the table arrangements. Tormaline, who liked to think of herself as older than her years, folded her hands like she'd had nothing to do with any of it.

Merry came back holding a small figure in her arms, about one fin tall. Esmerine recognized it instantly.

It was a statue of a winged person, springing from a tiny pedestal into the sky, wings lifted. Dosia took it from Merry and tried to give it to Esmerine.

Esmerine didn't take it at first. She glanced, ever so quickly, at Lalia Tembel, whose brow had furrowed with amusement. Then her eyes moved to her mother.

"Dosia, what on earth is that?" her mother said. "Where did you get it?"

"It's a statue of a winged person," Dosia said matter-of-factly. "I found it in the scavenge yard."

"Esme, do you still like winged boys, then?" Lalia said.

"No," Esmerine said. "I never *liked* winged boys." Not that it was much better, liking what Alander had brought—books with worlds tucked between their pages, stories about animals that spoke and brave youngest princesses—always the youngest, Esmerine noticed, never somewhere in the middle.

"You were just jealous, Lalia," Dosia said. "Everyone wished they were friends with Alander back then."

"I certainly didn't wish to be friends with Alander," Lalia said. Her mother nodded as she spoke. "I'm glad we can trade with humans, but nevertheless, land people have a certain aroma, and crude manners to match."

"Alander smelled like books!" Esmerine said.

"Oh, *that's* appealing."

"I mean, *dry* books."

"Don't bother," Dosia whispered in Esmerine's ear.

"It is a very finely crafted statue," said one of her father's friends. "You could get a good price for that from the traders, all right."

Esmerine stuck the statue behind her with the other gifts, and only after everyone had gone did she finally take it to her sleep room and study it, half with her fingers, by the faint light of glow coral. The figure was unclothed, neither boy nor girl, and unlike Alander, it lacked personality. It was like those winged people she sometimes saw far in the distance, hovering on the wind, leathern wings stretched wide.

Dosia slunk into the room they shared, jabbing Esmerine's tail with her elbow in the dim light. Not only did the cave lack light, but it lacked space. At least they didn't have to share with Tormy and Merry as well.

"Now Lalia Tembel is going to think I have some sort of obsession with winged people," Esmerine said. The gift was a nice thought, but only Dosia had really understood her friendship with Alander, and Esmerine wished she had not made an example of it at the party.

"Who cares what she thinks?" Dosia said. "Anyway, it's a lovely piece."

That was true enough. The lines were smooth and graceful and realistically proportioned. It was the finest thing Esmerine had ever owned. "You really found it in the scavenge yard?"

"Well . . . not really. I found it in a garden."

"What garden?"

"Oh . . . outside of the village." Dosia was maddeningly vague.

"Were you with Jarra?"

Dosia laughed once, almost nervously. "No, no."

She shifted close enough that bubbles tickled Esmerine's ear when she spoke. "Well, now that you're a siren too, I'll tell you, but you have to promise not to make a big fuss about it."

"Oh?"

"You know that big house on the rocks by the point?"

"Of course." Sometimes they both liked to sit on the rocks and watch the distant human house. On pleasant days, humans climbed down the path cut in the cliff with picnic baskets to eat on the rocky shore, and at dusk, lanterns glowed in the windows and intriguing shadows passed behind the curtains.

"I went inside it."

"*What?*"

"Shh! You'll wake Mother! Don't be so dramatic, I'm not going to do it anymore. It just happened. I was watching these young men on the rocks and suddenly one of them waved to me."

"And you went closer? That's the first thing they tell us not to do! What if he'd taken your belt?"

"He wouldn't do that. I was very careful—at first I stayed in the water and talked to them, but they were so nice, and so curious about me, that I promised them I'd come back. And when I came back, they asked if it was true that I could turn my tail into legs, and when I said it was, they offered me a dress."

All merfolk could turn their tails into legs if they wished, but every step shot pain from their heels. Only sirens could fully join the human world. If a human man stole their enchanted belt, or if they gave it willingly, the pain would cease, but they could never turn their legs to tails again. All mermaids grew up whispering stories of human men who beat wives, terrible food cooked over raging fires, unwashed bodies, and horses run amok. But it was also said that every human man yearned for a mermaid bride, and they loved more passionately than any man under the sea. Of course, they only said this when no mermen were around.

"I wanted to tell you," Dosia continued, "but you've been so busy these last couple of weeks, and the way Minnaray's been filling your head with all those human horror stories, I figured you'd overreact."

"Because it's dangerous," Esmerine hissed. "What if they're tricksters?"

"They're not *tricksters*," Dosia said. "You of all people should know not to believe rumors. Look at all the rumors people still spread about Alander."

"Well, but—Alander's different."

"We always did say we'd go to the human world together," Dosia said.

"Together," Esmerine agreed. She turned onto her side, facing the wall. That was what upset her most. Dosia had kept a secret.

"I knew I ought to tell you," Dosia said as if reading her mind. "I just . . . worried you wouldn't understand. And it happened so fast, and you weren't there—" She put a hand on Esmerine's shoulder. "Anyway, I hoped you'd like the statue. I admired it in the garden at the human house, and Fiodor—the young man—said I could have it. I was thinking of you. Wishing you were there. We should go back together."

"You truly think it's safe?"

"Perfectly. Fiodor and Giovan—that's the other one's name—are near our age, and they're both handsome, and I told them you might come later. We mostly stayed in the garden and by the shore. I could've run away anytime, or enchanted them with a song. No need to worry."

Their desire to see the surface world reached back to a time long before they had been chosen for siren's training. As children, they had talked a thousand times of going to the surface world, to marry humans if they felt romantic, to become the first female traders when they felt adventurous. Still, they weren't children any longer, and the elder sirens would disapprove of them spending time with humans.

"I don't know, Dosia . . . I took my oath today. It seems so soon."

"Oh, that's just tradition. Anyway, you never said you wouldn't associate with humans, just that you'd protect the sea from them. We aren't running away. We're only going to see their garden and house . . . their books . . ."

Esmerine had a weakness for books. When Alander had stopped visiting, books vanished from her life. If Esmerine truly believed Dosia was only interested in the garden or books, she would have agreed that moment. But something in Dosia's excited tone frightened her, made her want to steer her sister away from the human house perched on the rocks, just above the sea, so near and yet in another world entirely.

"Maybe later," Esmerine said. "You know how busy I'll be just now."

Usually, Esmerine went along with whatever Dosia wanted to do, but usually Dosia never kept secrets either, and Esmerine would not be convinced.

Chapter Three

Dosia typically slept latest of all the sisters, but the next morning Esmerine woke alone. She slunk into the main room, bleary from her fitful sleep. Her mother was cleaning up after last night's festivities, softly singing as she went. The room was still bright from the rented magic lights, which would be returned by afternoon.

"Mother, have you seen Dosia?"

"Isn't she sleeping?"

"No."

"Goodness. It's too early for her to be up and about. Don't tell me she has some new suitor."

Esmerine suppressed a twinge of anxiety. "I think her eye's been on Jarra."

Her mother smiled. "Jarra, really? He seems rather tongue-tied for our Dosia. But maybe that's what she likes about him."

"I think so. He'd listen to her talk all evening."

"Still, she won't marry a man like that, I hope," her mother said. "What woman really likes a husband with a jellyfish spine?"

"Oh, I don't know." Esmerine laughed a little. People sometimes commented that her mother was too bossy, her father too agreeable.

"What about you, my dear? You never say a word about boys, and you're almost a woman yourself! Or—not almost. You're a siren now. Goodness."

Esmerine edged toward the kitchen, hoping to distract herself with breakfast. "I don't know. I don't think I'll get married at all."

"I suppose the village can seem a very limited pool." Her mother waved her off. "Perhaps a traveler will grab your attention someday."

Esmerine ignored her. She had never been especially interested in boys. It was as if they all belonged to Dosia automatically, leaving her a quiet observer, which suited her fine most of the time.

Esmerine swam out to the bay, thinking she might find Dosia with the other sirens, but none of them had seen her either.

"She never comes this early," said Dosia's friend Alwina. "In fact, I'm surprised you're here now after such a night!"

"I didn't want to be late."

Alwina grinned. "That's just like you." Time was as fluid as the water in the mer world—the sun came up, the sun went down, and the moon changed phase, so when Alander told her about hours and clocks, she didn't know what he meant. In order to meet him, she had to change her thinking, to pay attention to a stricter rhythm. "But you certainly look lovely, and the parties are all over."

It was easy to stop thinking of Dosia amid the congratulations of the other sirens, who showered her with compliments and joked about parties past and how aggravating certain village elders were, always acting so puffed with importance on these occasions.

Siren magic had many uses—diverting warships from inhabited areas of the sea, for instance, or sinking whaling ships—but most days were spent in routine monitoring of the sea traffic. All the ships departing the great port of Sormesen sailed past the rocky point, where the bay completed its half-moon curve. A group of sirens kept watch there most hours of the day. The ships paid tribute to them, tossing a box overboard. The offering varied depending on the type of ship—gold was most common, but fishermen gave a portion of their catch, and some ships even gave kegs of wine. Mermen would fetch the tribute and blow a shell whistle once it was searched and found acceptable.

Esmerine knew from Dosia's stories that when the eldest sirens weren't present, the others would call to the sailors, especially the navy men in their great ships with tall masts and bright sails. The sirens would tease the small fishing boats to come nearer and nearer, almost within hands' reach, dashing beneath the waters at the last moment to stare at the hull above. Occasionally a fisherman would jump overboard to try and find them, and the sirens would scatter, laughing and shrieking. All sirens were fascinated by human men. The very quality that made their magic potent seemed to make them susceptible to the lure of the surface world.

Today Lady Minnaray and the other elder sirens were there, so the younger ones only gossiped and combed their hair. Morning turned into midday. The sirens shared fish the mermen brought.

"Where's Dosinia?" Lady Minnaray asked when Esmerine's sister didn't appear. "She was so excited for you to be sirens together, I'm surprised she isn't here on your first day."

"I suspect she's just . . . tired, from all the excitement." Esmerine didn't know why she was making excuses. Where *was* Dosia? The thought nagged at her, and she wanted to look for her, but she couldn't very well leave now without someone asking questions. And if Dosia had gone back to the human house, as Esmerine was beginning to suspect, she'd be furious if Esmerine told anyone.

In the afternoon, the sun reached its highest point, and the sea was a brilliant green blue at the rock and pure deep blue in the distance. Only Esmerine sat straight while the others sprawled on the rocks, singing old songs, occasionally dropping into the water when their scales began to dry out.

Esmerine imagined Dosia going to the human house, limping up the steps. The young men were waiting, leering, reaching for her—no, it wasn't the young men at all, it was an older man with a black moustache—a pirate. No, two pirates—one to grab her arms and the other to grab the belt from her waist . . . Dosia would cry for Mother and Father and Esmerine, and no one would hear her—no, Dosia would fight back and one would club her on the head—

Should Esmerine tell Lady Minnaray? But what if Dosia had simply snuck off with a friend—it wouldn't be the first time. All the fuss would be for nothing.

The life of a siren was easy most days, and Esmerine didn't wish to bring down a dangerous ship and drown humans, but she began to wish for something thrilling to happen to keep her from wondering about Dosia.

When Esmerine came home for dinner, Dosia was not there.

"Maybe she went to the scavenge yard with your father," her mother said. "Go tell them it's time to eat."

When human ships sunk on the rocks, whether from siren song, human error, or nature's wrath, professional scavengers brought the best loot to the elders to trade back to the humans. After they'd swept through, anyone might take the smaller pickings—weathered leather shoes, wooden spoons, fragile maps of the land that quickly fell apart.

Esmerine's father was a fisherman by trade, but a scavenger at heart. Whenever he had a holiday or a bountiful morning catch, he went straight to the ships' graveyard. Children used to scavenge too, but when Esmerine was a little girl, two boys had been killed when the wreckage of a ship collapsed on them, and now children were forbidden from entering the graveyard. Esmerine had sometimes been allowed to bring her father messages from her mother if something important happened, but that was only because she was careful to stay clear of the wrecks, whereas Dosia had gotten in terrible trouble once at the age of ten for ducking inside a ship to grab a perfectly intact china cup.

Now Esmerine was sixteen and allowed to come if she wished, but she still grew nervous as she drifted over the skeletons of ships. Sometimes she lost sleep worrying a ship might collapse on Father. She hated that Father came here, but she couldn't deny the fascination of the broken hulls that whispered ghostly secrets on the currents. Even when dozens of men and maids were picking through fresh wreckage, and the water grew dim with stirred sand, it was always eerily quiet. Out of respect for the dead, no one sang as they worked, as her father would while he caught fish. Today she only saw Wella and Triana, two older widows who scavenged for a living.

"Esmerine!"

She turned at the sound of Father's voice.

"Over here, my girl! Come here . . ." He ducked his head and arms through a broken window. His tail flicked, nudging him farther in.

"Be careful, Father . . ."

His grinning face ducked back out, and he held up a stubby top hat, dark gray with a black band. He clamped it on his head. "What do you think? It's in good shape yet. We can use it for theatricals."

Esmerine forced a smile. She couldn't think of theatricals without fretting about Dosia, with her talent for mimicking deep-sea accents and singing flirtations of comic songs, like "No More a Siren for Me." It wouldn't seem comical ever again if something happened to Dosia.

"Esmerine, dear? What is it? You seem troubled." He struggled to fit the hat in the bag at his waist. Through the loosely woven mesh, she saw that he'd already found a dented pewter plate and some small metal objects—spoons, possibly, or tools.

"It's Dosia. Have you seen her today?"

"Of course. She was up early with me," he said. "Said she was going to the rocks early."

"What rocks?"

"Well, I assumed she meant the sirens' rocks. She wasn't with you today?"

Esmerine had been nervous all day, but that seemed a feeble emotion compared to the terror now surging through her. "I haven't seen her at all."

"Oh," her father said, but now his voice was hushed, and he reached an arm to her. "Well, we'll find her. I'm sure she's not far." He drew her close to him, and she folded her head against his. She could feel her father's love for her, like warmth in the currents, like lights in the darkness.

"I'm worried . . . something happened to her," she said.

"What makes you think that?"

"She told me she went in a human house."

"Are you sure?" He stopped. "When have you girls been speaking to humans?"

"I haven't. Just Dosia. You know how she likes to sit on the rocks by the point."

"But . . . surely she has the sense to— You're *sure* she went in the house?"

"She told me last night. I would have told you, if I thought—" If something happened to Dosia, Esmerine would never forgive herself for not trying harder to convince her to stay away from the humans.

He smoothed her hair one last time. "We should tell your mother."

It was more difficult to tell her mother, because her mother overreacted to everything, and this was no exception. She gathered all the neighbors, even the ones she didn't care for, questioned everyone about whether they had seen Dosia, and before long a search party was combing the village for her. Esmerine began to dread Dosia's return almost as much as her disappearance—Dosia would be so mortified by all the commotion.

But Dosia did not come home that night. It was difficult to

search the sea in the darkness, but some of the traders went to the point to inquire about her at that grand house. Esmerine had never spent a night without Dosia, and she swam little circles in their cave, unaware that she had slept until she woke to the serious voice of a trader in the entry room.

Chapter Four

Esmerine slunk from her room to find her mother clutching Tormy's hand. Merry was likely still asleep, and her father must be out searching.

"They said they had no idea what we were talking about," the trader was saying. "But it might not be the truth. It was just a lad I spoke to first—must've been sixteen, seventeen. He seemed a little dumbstruck. But it doesn't mean he wasn't lying. You know what a prize mermaids are to humans."

"Did you *look* for her?" her mother said. "Of course you can't simply take his word for it!"

"I can't storm into a human gentleman's house and search it

up and down, madam," said the trader, a strapping man with a long bluish tail and a calm demeanor.

"But how am I ever going to know if they have my daughter?" Her mother was shaking Tormy's arm, apparently unaware she was even holding it.

"Sometimes . . . we lose sirens," he said carefully.

"Dosia wouldn't be that stupid!" Esmerine's mother snapped. "She's had it drummed into her head all her life to stay away from humans." Tormy managed to wrest her arm back from their mother's grasp as she started crying.

"I can send Lady Minnaray to speak with you, ma'am," the trader said. He lowered his head and touched his tail to the floor in a gesture of respect, then departed.

Yesterday, Esmerine had been frightened for Dosia, but today felt more like a dream. Dosia had always been fascinated by humans. Everyone expected her to be named a siren from a young age. And everyone knew sirens might follow their fascination with humans too far. When Esmerine was eight, they had lost a siren—an unmarried woman from a wealthy family. She had been out alone, taunted a fisherman, and he managed to grab her. At least, that was the story they were told.

Had Dosia been unhappy? Or was it something they had done? But Dosia had always seemed cheerful. Her only complaint was a yearning to see the surface world. Was that really enough to provoke her into such a dire act? No, surely she would have told Esmerine . . .

Esmerine recalled the trapped feeling that had closed around her when she made her siren's vow.

"If I'd known she was speaking with humans . . . !" Esmerine's mother sobbed.

"It's not your fault, Mother," Esmerine said. "You know how they say sirens become enchanted with humans. It's just an enchantment. It's no one's fault."

"Dosia and Esmerine always wanted to go be humans," Tormy said, her eyes flashing at Esmerine. "They were always putting on legs and showing off around the islands."

"You think this is my fault?" Esmerine cried. "Dosia didn't even tell me she was talking to humans!"

"Be silent, Tormaline!" Esmerine's mother shouted. "You could display at least one iota of pity for poor Dosia. It's one thing to walk about on an island as a child, and another to be kidnapped by a human man."

Tormy slashed the water with her tail. "Pity her? She should have known better! I miss her, but she's gone because she always liked humans better than anything else!" She fled the room.

Esmerine, too, returned to her sleep room and curled against the floor, clutching the winged statue to her chest. Her despair felt bottomless. There was no balm for Dosia's disappearance. She didn't even want to talk to her parents. She did feel guilty in some way—should she have tried harder to stop Dosia? If only Dosia hadn't gone to the human house without Esmerine in the first place, this wouldn't have happened. She still couldn't believe Dosia had done all this without her.

Esmerine kept replaying again and again the vision of Dosia being taken by human men, the gruff hand tearing Dosia's belt from her waist, the terror Dosia must have felt, knowing she'd been wrong about the humans and no one from home could help her.

Of course, everyone in the village knew Dosia was gone by day's end. Friends called, bearing gifts of sympathy. When Lalia Tembel and her mother came by, Esmerine said she was sick and hid in her room. Every time Esmerine passed one of Dosia's friends they would embrace her, and the tears would begin again. For a week, they had no theatricals, only songs of blessing for Dosia and mourning for themselves.

Esmerine continued her work as a siren, but Dosia's departure had drained the joy she should have felt. Fear for her sister twisted to anger and back again as she sat on the rocks with the other sirens.

Sometimes Esmerine found a solitary rock and watched birds fly overhead. She glimpsed winged people gliding on the western sky, near the mountainous cliffs they called the Floating City. She remembered how Dosia used to yell at Lalia Tembel for her, defending Esmerine's friendship with Alander. Now Dosia was experiencing things Esmerine couldn't even fathom, and worse, she didn't know if Dosia was all right.

For all that Esmerine and Dosia had dreamed of changing

their legs to tails and exploring the human world, Esmerine was sickened at the thought of her sister living the rest of her life with legs, sleeping close to a human man, talking only to humans and never again to her own people.

They would never be traders. They would never go looking for Alander together. They would never even be sirens together.

The world couldn't stop just because Dosia was gone. The other sirens urged Esmerine to go to a dance with them. Esmerine had always loved to sing and dance, and she had just begun to miss it, but it still felt wrong to enjoy herself. She lingered by the walls.

She noticed Jarra looking at her. He had always been nice to her, and he had bright black eyes and a quick smile. She lifted her face as he swam nearer.

"I was wondering . . . er . . . did Dosia say anything about me before she left?" he asked.

"Well . . . I know she liked your company."

"I really thought we might have a future together." He curled one hand into a loose fist. "I can't believe everyone's just sitting around when she's been kidnapped. Someone should go after her."

Esmerine agreed, but few merfolk could stand the pain in their transformed feet for long, and it was even more unlikely they would confront the humans, who would surely have hidden her belt well. Her sister was as good as a slave. Esmerine couldn't think about it. She wished Jarra would just leave her alone if he only wanted to talk about Dosia.

He noticed her crestfallen expression. "I'm so sorry."

"It's all right . . ."

"I know how close you two were."

"Yes . . . we were." Esmerine ran her fingers through the braids she had so carefully woven that morning. Dosia used to have a sure and willing hand with braids, but now Esmerine managed alone. Her mother and Tormy both yanked too hard.

Jarra bowed and turned to go, but she caught his arm. "You—you don't want to dance?" she asked, sounding more desperate than she intended.

"Oh. I didn't know you wanted to." He shrugged and pulled her into an awkward hold, but she imagined he was thinking of Dosia. Well, so was she, for that matter.

It was no better to be home. Her mother fretted all the time, wondering aloud how Dosia was doing. Tormy and Merry sang songs of how they might save her. The two younger girls even went to Olmera, the village witch, to ask if they might do something, and came back sulking and silent.

If Esmerine still knew Alander, he could have brought paper and helped her write Dosia a letter. Maybe he would have even flown around and looked for her. She asked the traders to look for him in the city.

"That winged boy? But I haven't seen him around in years," her father's friend told her. "He'll be all grown up."

"But he's—well—just see. He was tall for his age, and he always had a book. Brown hair a little lighter than mine, brown eyes too."

"All right. I'll ask. But those winged people all look the same."

Esmerine was now the oldest sister left, and more invisible than ever.

As weeks passed, life began to tingle back, and she wondered what would happen if she were to look for Dosia. Most merchildren tried walking once or twice, giving up after the first few twinges, but Esmerine and Dosia had persisted, bounding weightless on the ocean floor, standing on the shore of the tiny islands that dotted the bay, clutching rocks and trees for balance. Esmerine didn't think that the pain of walking could be worse than the pain of wondering where Dosia was.

Chapter Five

It was a daunting prospect, to imagine going after Dosia. Not only would her feet ache, not only would she be in an unfamiliar place, but even if she found her sister, the humans who had taken her belt surely wouldn't make it easy to get back. As much as her mother fumed at the traders, Esmerine understood they really couldn't help.

They needed someone who could move easily around the human world, someone clever who understood how things worked on the surface.

Someone like Alander.

She hadn't seen him in four years, but she knew he would remember her well. Their friendship had lasted for almost that long, and they had been the most memorable years of her life. Alander had driven her crazy half the time, bringing her chemises to wear while they played so she would be properly clothed, and preceding far too many statements with "Of course," making her feel stupid for asking questions. But he never failed to bring her a book, a different book every time unless she asked for an old favorite. He had taught her to read and write, scratching letters in the sand. She figured she knew as much about the human world as any trader, thanks to Alander's books and the things he told her.

His visits hadn't ended by choice. "I can't come anymore," he had said. "I have to go to the Academy."

"I thought you already went to school."

"That was just juvenile school. Father says I won't have free time anymore. I don't know what I can say. He still doesn't know I come to see you, and he'd be mad if he found out. But after I complete my studies at the Academy, Father says I'll work as a messenger for a year or two. I'll travel all over the country, so maybe I can visit you then."

Not long after that, he said a final good-bye and had never come again, although Esmerine kept waiting for his time as a messenger to begin. Esmerine knew from talking to the traders that many winged people worked as messengers, because they could travel faster than a horse or a ship. Esmerine supposed the work could have taken him to some far-flung direction. But it couldn't do much harm to look for him, at least.

She didn't know how to go about leaving, that was the

trouble. Besides the fact that her parents would never give their approval, she had promised Merry she'd help her practice for her school theatricals that week. She was the eldest sister now, and it seemed there was always so much to be done. Her family needed her.

One day, she was at the market with her mother and sisters when one of the traders came back with a rumor about a mermaid wife in Sormesen.

"I don't know if it's your girl," the man said. "But I don't know of any other merwives in Sormesen. They said the girl was beautiful but looked unwell, and that her husband was taking her to live in mountain country." He gave her mother a meaningful look. "They don't like the mermaids they steal to be too close to the sea. They think it makes 'em homesick."

Esmerine's mother stopped moving. She seemed afflicted by a sort of paralysis whenever anyone talked of how miserable Dosia might be. Esmerine and Tormy each took her by a hand and led her away.

"Oh, gods, gods, gods. It's Dosia, I just know it," she was muttering, and her hands started to play with her shell necklace.

"Mother," Esmerine said. "It's all right."

"If she had only resisted her impulses!" Mother cried. "She never would have been taken! And now she's moving farther and farther away. I can't bear having my girl so far away, and not even *knowing*—it's the not knowing that's going to send me to an early grave, I tell you!"

Merry's eyes were huge and alarmed, as if their mother

might really perish from her grief. Esmerine didn't think she would, but something had to be done.

"We have to bring her back," Esmerine said decisively. "Mother, please! Listen to me. I could go on land and find her. We know she was in Sormesen, and that she went to the mountains. If I could just get some information—"

"Esmerine, that is ridiculous. What if—what if it isn't even her? It could be a siren from another village."

"You know it's her."

"And you can't walk. I know you and poor Dosia used to play at it, but real walking—it's too much."

"I know I could. I used to play with Alander for hours. The pain isn't so bad, and I'm good at it. I can even climb trees. I could go to Sormesen and—at least I could bring word."

"We haven't the money for clothes and carriages and—"

"I'll sell all my bangles and hair beads and shells and I'll sell that statue Dosia gave me for my debut. I don't care about any of it. I just want to see her again."

Esmerine stayed calm. Her mother always responded to calm people, likely because she had such trouble keeping calm herself.

Her mother took Esmerine's hands and squeezed her fingers. "You really love your sister."

"Don't we all?"

"But . . . we can't just—go after her."

"We can too. There is no reason why I can't at least try. We'll regret it the rest of our lives if we don't *try*."

"Yes, we will. You are right about that . . ." Mother looked over her shoulder, as if searching for something. She sighed again. "I don't know what to do. I can't lose you both . . . but if Dosia needs us . . . Your father is hopeless on legs. The traders are absolutely useless."

"I know," Esmerine said, trying not to sound impatient. "That's why I have to go. I'll be careful. My siren magic will keep me safe, should anyone try to hurt me. I'll find Dosia."

Chapter Six

Esmerine thought her father would never let her leave, but even he admitted it would be reasonably safe for her to go to Sormesen and ask after Dosia. Besides, none of them would have any peace unless an attempt was made.

"Esmerine, you are a sensible girl," he said. "If anyone can find a way to bring Dosia home, I believe you would. Just be very careful and come back as quick as you can."

Esmerine draped all her beads on her neck and loaded her arms with bangles, trying not to think how she would soon give them all away. Clutching the winged statue close, she set off for the House of Decency.

Because merfolk didn't wear clothes, the humans required them to stop at a certain point on the outskirts of the city where they could rent the proper attire for venturing on land. Like every young mer, Esmerine had swum close enough to the House of Decency to gaze at it from afar, and also like every young mer, she was disappointed the place didn't look more exciting. Beyond the sandy beach, a small wooden house with arched windows sat between two tall wooden walls. A weathered sign with a painted picture of a shirt and breeches hung from the left wall.

Esmerine pumped her tail forward until the water was no deeper than the length of her body, and then she forced the change. She had gotten much better at it over the years, but it was never pleasant. She doubled over as her very bones shifted. Her long fins drew themselves up into tight, dense little feet, then spread into toes that barely glanced the sandy ocean floor, sending a faint, almost ticklish pain across her newborn soles.

Even though the shore was lonely, Esmerine made a point not to show even a hint of pain as she placed one foot in front of the other and her head emerged from the water, her hair clinging to her back and breasts in tendrils. Dull pain shot from her feet to her knees with every step. She'd heard traders compare it to knives, but it never felt like that to her. The ache was familiar, almost welcome, for she associated it with better days, before Alander and Dosia had disappeared.

It felt, she thought, like heartbreak, only physical. Like

she was tearing apart from the sea with each step. She almost expected it would vanish if she could only put enough distance between her body and the rush of waves.

Her body felt heavy in the air. Every bangle and bauble suddenly weighed on her neck and her arms. Only her golden siren's belt still seemed to rest gently against her skin. She trudged across the shore, adjusting her balance as the sand shifted under her feet. By the time she reached the blue door of the House of Decency, she had to force herself not to grit her teeth.

"Hello!" she called. The snarling face of some unknown beast stared out at her from the center of the door, a large brass ring clutched in its mouth. Esmerine was wondering if she was supposed to pound on it when the door swung open and a young man did a double take at her before shouting behind him, "Madam!"

He turned back to her, cheeks red. His eyes dropped to her breasts and quickly up to her face again. Esmerine flushed in return. Humans seemed to treat bodies like nasty secrets, and she felt that way when she formed legs.

"She'll be along shortly, if you'll wait there," he mumbled. Esmerine hardly understood his accent. "We don't get many lady mermen. I mean, mer ladies."

"That's all right," Esmerine said, but he was already rushing off. A woman almost immediately came striding along. Her long face reminded Esmerine of a porpoise, only not so friendly. Her clothes were stiff and ruffly, and she moved accordingly.

"A mer girl," she said, with a note of surprise that did not extend to her stern expression. "A siren, at that. How odd. Well, you can't stand there like that. Come along. Did you bring those bracelets to trade?"

"Yes."

"Very well." She shot a look at the servant boy, who was standing in the hall. "Tell my husband I'm dealing with the girl and he is not to get involved."

"Yes, madam." He scurried off.

Esmerine followed the woman into a narrow hall that reeked of human—a thick, ripe odor of smoke and sweat and roasted meat. Her bare feet picked up a film of invisible grime from the cool tile floors. She winced at the woman's pace but didn't dare to slow down. Clothes and fabrics filled the small room where they stopped, some in folded piles and some hanging on hooks. There were stubby top hats, and little funny shoes with buckles, and dark coats with tails, and white linen shirts, and breeches. Men's clothes. The woman knelt on the floor, opening a trunk full of colors pale and bright and girlish, and she rummaged through them.

"What brings you here, then?" she asked. "Not content singing on rocks, are you? You're coming on land to steal the men now?"

"I'm looking for my sister."

The woman held up a thin linen shift, like the one Alander used to make her wear. "Hold up your arms. Your sister? Is she a merwife? You won't get her back."

"I just want to see what's become of her."

"You want a human husband," the woman said, tugging the shift over Esmerine's body. "Otherwise you wouldn't be a siren."

"How do *you* know?" Esmerine couldn't hold back her irritation.

The woman brought a stiff bodice out from the trunk. "We know all about your kind here. A few men in Sormesen have married mermaids. They come to us thinking we know what to do because we talk to the merfolk. The men are too blinded by enchantments to see they've married fools who hide from the fire, can't handle the servants, and complain about every little thing." She drew the bodice over Esmerine's shoulders and stood behind her, tugging the laces tight.

Esmerine gasped. "I can't breathe." The bodice seemed to be made of slender rods sewn into the fabric that pushed her breasts up and drew her waist into an unnatural tapered shape. She'd been fascinated by Alander's books, with their pictures of human ladies with tiny cone-shaped torsos and frilly gowns, but she had never believed real human women could resemble the drawings.

"If you truly couldn't breathe, you wouldn't be talking either," the woman said. "This is what I mean. I don't know why a mermaid would want to come here, when you complain merely at wearing stays."

"You don't seem to like mermaids very much." Esmerine wondered why the woman sounded so hostile. She only wanted to rent a dress and then she would be gone.

"Why would any sensible woman like mermaids?" the woman said, incredulous. "You wreck our ships to frighten us. You run about naked with your horrid fish tails and sing all day to seduce our men."

"We only wreck ships that don't pay tribute, and it's only fair when they're taking fish from our ocean, and I certainly don't care to seduce your men!"

The woman shot her a look of poison, giving the laces of the stays a hard tug. "Nor do you know when to hold your tongues."

Esmerine did hold her tongue as the woman trussed her from head to toe—a padded roll around her hips, a striped cloth overbodice that fitted against the stays, a pale green underskirt and carefully draped overskirt of darker green, stockings, shoes with heels that made Esmerine's pained feet wobble, and a bonnet trimmed with black ribbon and still more lace that tied under Esmerine's neck with a choking knot. Esmerine still felt her siren's belt beneath her clothes, reminding her she was still a free mermaid at heart. It was hard to think that Dosia might wear these clothes forever.

"For payment, your bracelets will do," the woman said.

"All of them?" Esmerine had a strong sense she was being cheated.

"Yes, they're nothing too fine. What is that you have there?"

Esmerine had put down the statue of the winged figure, but now she snatched it up again. She didn't want to sell it to this woman who hated mermaids. "Nothing."

The woman peered closer at it. "Ugh. One of those winged

folk. One of them snatched my aunt's hat right off her head with his horrible long toes. I never thought much of them since. Well, let me see your beads. I imagine you'll want to trade something for a ride into town."

The servant boy took Esmerine into town. Esmerine sat next to him on the wooden seat, but the sides of her bonnet concealed him from her view unless she made a point to turn her head toward him. She could see his hands holding the reins. Large, tanned hands with a cut along the back of the left. She'd never been so close to a human man, and she could feel him looking at her and could smell his sweat. The sun beat on her arms and the back of her neck, exposed between bonnet and collar, and she felt her own sweat trickling between her breasts.

The cart bumped along, rattling and jarring over the road and in Esmerine's ears. Except for the lovely sharp sounds of porpoises and the bark of seals, sounds underwater were softer and fluid. Everything here seemed loud and sped up. Esmerine gripped the side of the cart, but pulled back at the way it vibrated under her hand. She reminded herself not to be afraid. This was the human world she'd always longed to see. These were the horses—certainly larger than she envisioned—that she swore she wouldn't be frightened of.

The cart jolted suddenly, and the boy grabbed her shoulder. She looked at him, and he took his hand back. "All right, miss?" His dark brows furrowed with concern.

"Of—of course."

He kept looking at her, and he grinned just a little, and then he seemed shy again. "Tell me if you need anything."

"All right." She turned her head away again. The clothes made her feel very fragile, like some human-made thing that would break apart and dissolve underwater, and now this human boy was looking at her like mermen never did. It was like a curious kind of game.

Along the path to Sormesen, the sea glittered between buildings of two and three stories that were topped with red tile roofs. The breezes blew a fresh scent across the city, but even so, the aromas of dung and urine crept into Esmerine's nose. They had to stop as a leathery old woman herded sheep across the road. Men, women, children, dogs, horses, and chickens all contributed to the traffic that grew thicker in the city. She heard someone shout over the din, "Spare a coin! Spare a coin!" She turned to see a man, so grimy that she couldn't guess at his age, waving stumps of arms in the air. "Spare a coin!"

She gasped and looked away, meeting the eyes of the boy driving the carriage again. He patted her arm. "Beggars, miss. You don't have beggars below seas?"

"Not in my village. The elders take care of people who are sick or maimed if their families can't, but I've—I've never seen anyone so . . . hurt."

"Poor thing," he said. Esmerine thought he meant the beggar until he said, "Your world must be wonderful to produce such a kind and beautiful creature."

She didn't know what to say to that. What would Dosia have said? Would she flirt, or scold him for such a comment? Or would even Dosia be tongue-tied here?

The moment to respond came and went, but he didn't seem to mind. He began to whistle over the clamor of people shouting the merits of their hot rolls or dried fish or pamphlets, the woman standing in her doorway pounding the dust from a rug, the grunts and whines of animals. Esmerine had never realized just how many humans lived in Sormesen. There seemed as many people in view as lived in her entire village, and the spires and towers she had seen distantly from the water loomed impossibly high in person. Her mind scrambled through her memories, trying to connect the things before her eyes with the pictures and stories in Alander's books. Could she ever find Alander or Dosia among so many people?

"Um . . . excuse me."

She had thought the boy wasn't paying attention to her anymore, but the moment she spoke, he turned alert eyes her way. "Yes?"

"Do you know where the winged folk gather around here?"

The boy glanced at the statue on her lap. "Winged folk?" He squinted doubtfully.

"Yes."

"The messenger station, I guess."

"Could you take me there?"

He frowned slightly but squinted ahead like he was thinking of how to change his route to get her there. The cart continued forging through the crowds and turned down a street hemmed by walls of tan stone with climbing vines that seemed to give up halfway. Esmerine thought it couldn't possibly get any more crowded but it did. People didn't even try to get out of the way of the horses; there was nowhere else to go.

"Is it always like this?" she asked.

"We're nearing the market," he said. "It's that time of day when everyone's rushing about."

They finally made it into a rectangular clearing paved with flat stones, surrounded by buildings of four and five stories, even one with a bell tower. A colossal pillar rose from the center of the square. Following the line of the pillar, a winged figure suddenly shot into the air with papers gripped in his toes, one of which slipped free and fluttered into the crowd below. He hovered in the air a moment before dropping back to the ground again, like a gull swooping upon its prey.

Esmerine clutched her heart through the rigid stays. For a moment, she thought it was Alander, and resisted an urge to leap from the carriage. But no, Alander had been taller even when she last saw him.

"Can we stop here? I want to speak to him, just for a moment," Esmerine said, putting down the winged statue and turning toward the side of the cart.

"Of course," the boy said. "I'll help you down."

He hopped from the cart and ran around to her side, where he placed his strong hands around her waist and whisked her down like she was still near-weightless underwater. She braced herself for the pain of her feet hitting the ground and managed not to wince, but she limped as she approached the winged boy.

The boy looked around Tormy's age—twelve or thirteen— with hair to his chin and scruffier clothes than she recalled Alander wearing. He shouted to the passing crowd, "The newest pamphlet from Hauzdeen! Hauzdeen's views on royalty! Sir? Madam?" He waved a wing at a passing couple who were overdressed for the heat. They shook their heads.

Alander had always depised nicknames like "bird-boy," for the winged folk looked nothing like birds. The boy's wings resembled a leather cape draped over slender arms, but he had no hands, only a thumb and finger. What might have been his other three fingers stretched to form the framework of his wings. The thin skin of his wings attached at his sides, down to his knees, and his blue vest and brown knickers seemed to fit around him like magic, but she knew from Alander that the winged folk customarily pierced their skin in three places where their wings met their torsos, eventually forming holes just large enough for a fastener to slip through and hold the fronts and backs of clothing together. She had always found the idea clever yet disgusting.

The winged boy perked up when he noticed her studying him. "Say, you look like an intelligent young lady. Surely you'd like to read Hauzdeen's views of royalty?" He thrust a pamphlet her way.

"No, thank you, I—"

"I don't blame you. I don't understand a word in this

pamphlet," the boy said, fanning himself with the papers. "But maybe you'd like to buy one to use as a fan yourself?"

"No, I just wanted to ask if you happened to know a boy— man—" she stammered, reminding herself Alander would have aged just as she had. "Someone named Alander."

"If you mean Alan, sure. He works at the bookshop."

"Is he a Fandarsee too?" The winged folk called themselves Fandarsee—which, Alander once explained, meant "winged folk" in the Fandarsee trade tongue.

"That he is, miss. And if you're interested in him, you'll certainly want to purchase this pamphlet because he *loves* to discuss it. Say, isn't that your husband driving off?"

Esmerine whirled just in time to see the cart and the boy and the winged statue trotting off into the throng. "He's certainly not my husband!" she exclaimed. "Oh no." She tried going after the cart, but her shoes pinched her toes and her heels wobbled. She should never have left the statue alone, even for a moment.

The winged boy hurried up to her. "Wait, stop! Who is he, then?"

"He just gave me a ride into town, and he has a statue I brought to trade. I don't have many more things left!"

"Wait here." The boy leaped into the sky, spreading his wings. Years had not dulled the thrill that ran through Esmerine when she saw one of the winged folk break free of the world's pull. They could not take flight on the power of their wings alone, Alander had told her. They were built for gliding, but they cultivated magic for lifting themselves off the ground, harnessing the wind, defying the laws that held everything in place.

The horse cart had vanished around a building, but the winged boy would be able to see it from his vantage point in the sky, and he hovered a moment before he dove, disappearing beneath the rooftops.

Alander. Alan. Did this boy work for Alander? Her Alander—it must be so. Unless it was a common name. She shouldn't get her hopes up.

The boy appeared above the building again, clutching something in his toes. He swept over her, scattering leaves across the stones with the rush of his wings, bowing as he landed, passing the statue from foot to wing. He brought it over to her, beaming. "There you go, miss."

Tears hovered perilously close to her eyes, both from gratitude and from the sheer wonder of seeing a flying boy again. "Thank you."

"If you'd like to see Alan, he's probably at the bookshop. It's down Cerona Street." The boy pointed across the square. The distance looked eternal, and now she had no moony-eyed boy and horse cart. Damn her feet.

"How far?" she asked.

"You're a mermaid, aren't you?"

"Is it that obvious?" Esmerine didn't like to think everyone who saw her knew she was a mermaid.

"Somewhat, but especially to me, because a mermaid runs

the bookshop." He frowned. "Mermaid? Maybe mercrone would be better."

An older mermaid? Running a human bookshop? Esmerine was surprised she'd never heard of it before, and she wasn't sure Alander would be working for a mermaid.

"It'd be too far for you, I think." The boy gave her the briefest sympathetic look.

"I want to try. This Alan you work with . . . is he young? Eighteen or nineteen?"

The boy made a face. "Oh, he's young, but he acts like he might as well be some old uncle."

That sounded like Alander all right. "Tell me how to get there."

The boy gave her directions and wished her luck. If she could just make it . . . Alander would surely help her find Dosia. He'd understand. He'd played with Dosia too.

She must not think of her feet. She had to learn to ignore pain. She just had to put one foot in front of the other. Hundreds of times.

Chapter Seven

Cerona Street angled upward, and every step dragged at her feet until they burned with pain. Behind panes of rippled glass, shops displayed watches and little jeweled boxes and bonnets like the one she wore, only nicer, by the looks of it. She tugged at the ribbon under her neck again, loosening it. If only she could do the same for her stays. She wasn't used to wearing anything, and now she couldn't so much as wiggle. Sweat trickled under her arms. If only she could duck under the water and free herself of her trappings, but there was no water in sight, only dusty streets that made her thirsty just to look at.

She only had to make it to the bookshop. To Alander.

She found herself thinking back again to his departure. *Father doesn't know I come to see you, and he'd be mad if he found out.* Did his father have anything to do with the bookshop? Would he still be mad?

Up ahead, a wooden sign displayed a picture of a book. It spurred her on, and she reached the building rather quickly, only to encounter a scrawled note posted on the door that said *Be back at half past.*

Esmerine tried to remember exactly what that meant, when she hadn't heard Alan speak of measuring time in years. Half past an hour? Yes. And an hour wasn't all that long.

Even so, she knocked on the door and pressed her face to the windows. A wooden counter and shelves sat in the shadows along the far walls. Were those shelves all full of books?

No one came. Her feet hurt too badly to think of taking another step. She sunk onto the worn stones beneath her to wait.

So tired . . . She couldn't think about how tired she was. She pulled off her slippers with a groan and rubbed her aching soles. She couldn't wonder what she would do if Alander never came, if Alan wasn't Alander. She couldn't imagine walking all the way back to the square and starting her search for Dosia now. She put her hand to the siren's belt at her waist, murmuring songs under her breath, hoping to draw a little strength.

People passed, most of them paying her no attention even as she watched them—girls in dirtied aprons and leather shoes, old men with bent backs, travelers with paper-pale skin burned by the sun. She had yet to see the same person twice. Maybe she never would. How did you get to know anyone, among so many people?

She'd know Alander, though. Years had passed, but not so many years. She remembered his fleeting, flashing smiles, the dark gleam of his eyes. They'd share old memories, talk of old times.

A man. Alander would be practically a man now. She'd known it, but suddenly she realized he'd look different, not just taller. He might have sideburns and a hat like the passing humans; he had a job, for all she knew he could be married—

Gods knew who he might be now.

When he finally came, it seemed like a dream. He wore the brim of his short beaver-felt hat tugged low over his eyes against the sun. He had an open book between his fingers, reading as he walked, just like old times, but he was not the fourteen-year-old boy she remembered at all. He had grown tall and graceful—at least as graceful as one could be dodging a pile of horse droppings while one's nose was buried in a book—and he looked quite good with sideburns.

He peered at her above the book cover some moments after she noticed him. He quickly snapped the book shut and shoved it within his vest, leaving an awkward rectangular shape there. "Good afternoon, miss—" He doffed his hat. She'd almost forgotten his accent, clipped, like he was in a hurry to get the words out and go. "I'm sorry. I just had a brief errand to run. What are you looking for today?"

He didn't even recognize her!

She rose to her feet, pushing her hair back behind her ears, waiting for it to dawn on him.

He stepped closer. His eyes filled with sudden shock. Oh, thank the waters!

"Esmerine?" he said, slowly replacing his hat on the back of his head.

"Yes. It's me." A flutter rushed from her stomach to her throat. Oh dear oh dear. Alander. He was real. She didn't know what else to say. She hadn't realized how different they'd be now. Of course she hadn't really expected to find a boy, but she also hadn't realized she'd find a man of Sormesen with a hat to doff and a necktie. His cropped bangs clung to his forehead in the heat. He was taller than her by a good half a fin, where they had once been nearly the same height. He came very close to her, close enough that she smelled the smoke and fire of the human world on his clothes.

"You—you . . ." His lips moved a moment without any words coming out, like he spoke only to himself. "You didn't come to . . . to find me, did you?"

"No. I'm looking for my sister."

He breathed, his surprise slipping away, replaced by the old Alander she knew, drawn up and proper. "Dosia? Here? Well, why don't we go in and have a drink and you can tell me the whole story. There must be a story."

He didn't wait for an answer. He took a ring of keys from inside his vest and let them in. The shelves, she saw now, were indeed full of books—hundreds, thousands. Esmerine had only ever seen one book at a time before. Of course all those books Alan brought had to come from somewhere, but she never realized . . .

Alan hung his hat on a peg, atop a black cloak already hanging there. He scratched his back on the door frame. He straightened out a few books on a display table. She watched all this without a word, wondering if he'd ever stop moving. It was almost like he was avoiding her.

Finally. He nudged a chair toward her and sank into the other himself, taking the book out from his vest.

He watched her limp to the chair, a funny expression in his eyes, like pity—or guilt . . . ? She didn't want Alan to pity her, like she pitied the beggars on the street. He had seen her walk before, on the islands, and even work her way up trees, and he hadn't pitied her then. She suddenly felt stupid.

He looked out the windows, fixating on a girl trying to urge a pig down the street with little success. "What happened to your sister?"

She had long imagined this moment, when she would see Alander again. They would tell each other everything, say things like:

I've never forgotten you.

Nor I you.

Her memories of him had been so different. Maybe he just wasn't suited to the city, she decided. It seemed like he had something else on his mind.

She didn't really want to tell him anything now. She instantly sensed that she would only be a burden to him. Yet, something had to be said. "Yes, Dosia . . . well, we think she's been taken by a human man. She was a siren."

"And you came after her?" he said, turning back to her sharply. "If she's bound to a human man, you can't do anything for her."

"At the very least I need to bring word of her back home."

"Would you really be content just to bring word?" Alander asked, in the snappish tone she remembered all too well when something irritated him. She wondered suddenly why she ever wanted to see him again.

"Look, Alander, it's Dosia. I have to try. If I never even *tried* . . . She'd do the same for me."

Alander looked restless sitting down. "Well." He tapped his thumbs together. "I understand . . ."

"Do you?" She tried not to sound especially hopeful.

"Where are you staying? For how long?"

"Nowhere . . . yet." She tried to smile, like she had it all planned. "I have this statue to trade for lodgings."

He squinted. "Let me see."

She passed it to him, and he frowned. "It's one of us."

"Well, yes."

"It looks . . . rather like it's from the Second Imperial period. My father collects these. Strange thing for a mermaid to have."

"I don't know. Dosia gave it to me."

He put it down, still regarding it. "You'll have to take it to market and trade for coins, then make your way to an inn, and then go who knows where looking for your sister."

"I can walk," she said, sounding much more capable than she felt.

"In a manner of speaking." He looked up as two girls stepped inside the shop. "How can I help you ladies?"

They turned their bonneted heads to one another, giggling. One shook her head.

"We have a new pamphlet by Hauzdeen," Alander said.

"Hauzdeen?" one of the girls said, fluttering dark eyelashes. "I don't think I've read anything he's written."

"It's a bit controversial, but his arguments are very well posed, and I think any reasonable person will see he considers both sides," he said, thankfully unmoved, Esmerine thought, by the plump and healthy girl whose big blue eyes matched her dress. "I'm sure you'll find it enriching."

"I have all the enriching I need," the other girl said. "Do you have any new Verrougian novels? Along the lines of *A Courtesan and a Gentleman*?"

He sighed, not at all imperceptibly or good-naturedly, and moved to one of the shelves, taking down a book with a deep-red cover. "Lousan's latest. *Isabella*. I've heard it is *very* much like *A Courtesan and a Gentleman*."

"Then that is exactly what we want," the girl in blue said, taking coins from her purse. Alander wrapped the book in paper, and with one last giggle, they left, swinging their little purses.

Alander sank back in his chair, tapping the cover of his book with a finger. He glanced at the counter, where a piece of paper lay, *Alan* written quite clearly at the top. Esmerine noticed it said, between ink spatters, "Sweep the floors" and "Fix mess in poetry." He snatched it up, frowned, and put it down again.

"People are so tedious," he said. He turned back to her. "You won't get very far on your own. But I'm very busy working here at the shop."

It didn't seem the best idea to ask for his help just now, but she needed him. "Could I do anything in the shop? In exchange for your help?" Her eyes roamed back to the books lining the walls. They enticed her with their spines—some tall and promising pictures, some crumbling and requiring a delicate touch, some just the right size to hold in a hand, with pretty gilt titles.

He waved an almost scolding finger. "Oh, there's nothing you can do. Certainly you have no experience in a bookshop." He leaned his head into his fingers and pinched his forehead. "What am I saying? I can't very well refuse to help an old friend, can I?"

Such reluctance. No, indeed, she was a burden, and she couldn't bear that. She got to her feet as fast as she could. "Never mind, Alander, I can find Dosia myself. I never expected to come across you in the first place, after all." She stalked to the door, her movements jerky, but the pain wasn't just in her feet now. She'd been naive to think of him all these years, she saw that now, but—

He was on his feet in a flash, sweeping behind her. "Esmerine—wait."

"I don't need your pity. I didn't come looking for you, like I said. I just figured it was worth asking. Maybe I don't have experience, but I would never ask you to help me without offering something in return." She clenched the skirts that clung to her legs and hindered her steps. She was letting pride get in the way of looking for Dosia, and that wouldn't do, but none of this was going as she had planned.

"No, I'll look for Dosia," he said. "Tell me where I might find her."

"I don't know," Esmerine said, still upset. Even now, he didn't sound apologetic for taking such a snappish tone. "We thought she'd gone to the big house on the point. The one made from tan stones that looks like a castle. But the humans there denied they'd ever seen her. Now we've heard a rumor that her husband has taken her to mountain country."

"I know the house," he said, reaching for his hat. "I'll go investigate."

"You don't have to go this very moment! Anyway, I wondered if I could hire a cart to take me there." She didn't want to send Alander alone. He didn't seem especially passionate about Dosia's fate, and she feared he wouldn't ask the right questions.

"I ought to see what I can find out before you bother with a cart. Don't worry. I imagine they'll be more likely to answer me than a mermaid. It shouldn't take more than an hour, and Swift will return before I do."

"Thank you, Alander." Even if he didn't really want to help her, she meant it heartily.

"It's nothing." He paused. "You can call me Alan now. Humans have first and last names from birth, so I broke mine into two, Alan Dare. Fandarsee don't take last names until they've chosen a profession. And only my father calls me Alander anyway."

"Alan, then. Or should I say Mr. Dare?"

"Alan."

"Thank you, Alan." She smiled, but he didn't smile back.

She watched him go, but didn't have the pleasure of watching him take flight; he walked out of sight first. She turned back to explore the bookstore, but her feet still hurt badly from the walk, so she picked up the book Alan had been reading and dragged a chair to the window to wait. Maybe she could read a chapter or two and discuss it with him when he returned. *On Morality* had chapter titles like "The Nature of Man" and "Consciousness and Dreams." She started to read a little, but none of it made much sense. If only it did. She had so much catching up to do with books.

It felt strange to sit in a chair. One didn't really need chairs underwater. Her stays kept her sitting very rigidly, and her stockings itched. She was out of the sun, but out of the breeze too. Could the windows open? It looked like they might, but she wasn't sure how. Couples strolled by, consulting maps; a group tromped along in funny little black hats with red feathers; children played tag and screamed with laughter she could hear through the glass.

An older man with white hair poufing from a bald spot poked his head in. "Are you open for business, miss?"

"Um—no. Alan will be back at half past." She motioned to the sign.

"Funny, I was here earlier and it said the same. I'm sure that was a different hour. Who are you, then?"

"I'm just . . . a friend of his."

"Miss Belawyn's not here today either?"

Esmerine assumed Belawyn to be the mysterious mermaid owner. "I guess not."

"Well, do you mind if I look around?" The man stepped in and headed for the shelf without waiting for permission. "I'll be no trouble at all. In fact, I'll be glad enough to look without Mr. Dare hovering over me every moment, suggesting I read Hauzdeen and Ambrona and Volcke, and sniffing when I'd rather have something enjoyable that doesn't make my head throb."

"What do you like to read?" It was an irresistible novelty having a conversation about books with a stranger.

He browsed a moment, and took one out. "Now, this author is excellent. He's working on a complete history of the ancients, and this is the latest volume. Gripping history." He noticed her eager expression and handed her a different book. "This is the first part. You'd want to start with it."

She opened it to a plate in the front with a picture titled *The Oracle at Sormesen*. A wide-eyed woman held out her arm to an alarmed-looking man in some kind of lightweight armor. Other women were clustered behind him, looking equally alarmed. "*If the sorcerer ascends the throne, fire will rain down upon the empire,*" read the text at the bottom.

"My dear, you look as if that book is an old friend you haven't seen in a decade."

She shut it and smiled sheepishly. "I just get excited about books."

"Then you're in the right place, aren't you?" He patted the cover of the first book. "I'll likely purchase this one, but I'll browse until Alan returns."

Esmerine returned to her chair. She felt the man watching her careful steps, but he said nothing. She opened the history book and looked at all the pictures first. The merfolk didn't have pictures. No written word. The only way to share stories was by song and movement and passing tales from one mouth to another. When Esmerine was younger and her grandmother was still alive, she used to love to help her in the kitchen and listen to story after story.

The very first time Alan came, he carried a bucket for gathering seaweed clutched in his toes, and a book tucked into his vest. She had been playing near the islands as he swept down, and she hid behind the rocks and watched him as he filled the bucket a quarter full with seaweed, and then sat on the shore holding the curious red square to his face. At that time she had never even seen a book before. Sometimes they were in the wrecked ships, but she was too young to go there, and books had no value as salvage. She thought he was using it as a shield against the sun, but she could see him turning the pages and wondered what they were.

It wasn't long before she gathered the courage to approach him. She didn't change her tail into legs. She was just shy of her ninth birthday and far from adept at walking. She crawled forward in the sand and he looked up and asked who she was.

The very first thing she asked, after they had exchanged names, was what he was holding, and the very first thing he had done was to explain to her about books and writing. He told her that even her name could be written down, and he wrote it in the sand with a stick. After he was gone, she tried to copy it over and over, mesmerized by the idea that a vast story could be quietly contained, permanent and unchanging. Alan had read some of the book to her, so she knew the story in the book could be told aloud, just like her grandmother's stories, but it could also be a private story, read quietly to oneself. Esmerine had private stories in her head sometimes, but if she forgot them before a night of songs and theatricals, or if there was no time that night for her story, it was gone forever.

"Is this real?" she asked the older man now, pointing at a picture of odd spotted beasts.

"Those are giraffes. Yes. They're real. We don't have them in Sormesen, of course. I believe there is one in the menagerie in Torna."

Esmerine nodded, satisfied enough that such funny crea-
tures truly existed.

The door opened again. For a moment, she saw wings and
a hat and thought Alan had returned, but the man was silver
haired, wearing spectacles and a collar stiff enough to touch his
cheeks. A woman came just behind him, in a fine cape pinned
with a jeweled brooch, probably to cover the shirt and britches
that humans would undoubtedly consider immodest.

"Where is Alan?" the man demanded.

"He'll be back at half past," Esmerine said. For people with
regular access to books, everyone in Sormesen certainly had
trouble reading.

"Well, where is he? Don't tell me he's off gallivanting in coffee shops now?"

"Uh—"

"Who are you? A relative of Belawyn's?"

"Um—"

"Why are you here?"

Esmerine had an instinctive sense that it wouldn't be wise to
tell the truth. "I'm just an acquaintance passing through, mind-
ing the shop for a moment."

"Well, I don't have time to dither around and wait for him.
I've got appointments to keep. Tell him I was here and I'll
certainly be back."

"It isn't long until half past," the woman said.

"Long enough! No, I've got better things to do. Anyway,
when he learns I was here he'll know what I want to talk about

and will have time enough to mull it over, or better yet, come straight home."

The winged boy from the square walked in then, his wings folded around the Hauzdeen pamphlets, but he looked like he wanted to step right back out when he saw the older couple.

"Say, boy, have you seen Alander?"

"I have a name," the boy said, moving past him and dumping the pamphlets on the counter.

"Oh, Swift? Some sort of carnival name? It's rather shameful." As the man spoke, the woman sucked air through her teeth like she wished he would quiet down.

"Well, it's the only name I've got," Swift said, now stacking the pamphlets, more as a distraction than anything, it seemed. "And I haven't seen Alander, but I assume he'll be back at *half past*."

"The manners of an urchin," the winged man muttered, heading for the door. He looked at Esmerine one last time. "You'll tell him I was here?"

"I will."

The man and woman left. Esmerine glanced at Swift, but he was already asking the other man if he needed anything. Swift took the man's money for the history book and made a note in the accounts. "Good day, sir," he said, back to his cheerful salesboy persona.

"Good day."

The door shut. Swift flipped the coin the human had paid

with and caught it, three times in a row, then dropped it in the coin box. "So you found the place," he said.

"I did. Was that Alan's father?"

"Yes. Did you tell him you know Alan?"

"No."

"Smart. He doesn't like anybody." Swift sat behind the desk and kicked his feet up on the counter, flexing his toes. Fandarsee didn't have the feathered wings of a bird, but their feet were shaped similarly for grasping something while in flight, with long toes and a small thumb on the back of their heel. "How do you know Alan anyway?"

"It was a long time ago," Esmerine said. "We were kids. He used to come to the islands and gather seaweed and we talked." She spoke quickly, leaving emotion behind. Alan had seemed so unimpressed by her appearance after their years apart, so she didn't want to make much of it either. "Why was his father here? He sounded upset."

"He's *always* upset," Swift said. "Whenever he visits we'd all rather be somewhere else. He loaned the shop some money a while ago and it hasn't all been paid back. I think he loaned the money so he could keep some kind of tie on Alan. He's that kind of person. But I wouldn't care if Alan did go. I guess he used to be your friend, but I can tell you that he's a pompous—"

The door opened again, and this time it was Alan. Swift yanked his feet from the counter. Alan hung up his hat again and looked at Esmerine.

"I went to the house," he said. "I spoke to a young man there, who said a Lord Carlo had been visiting him when a mermaid came and 'charmed' them, and gave Lord Carlo her belt. He was not entirely forthcoming with this information, mind you, but I managed to get it out of him."

"Charmed them? No, they must have stolen it from her!"

"I'm sure you're right; I'm only telling you what he said."

"Thank you," Esmerine said, tugging at her clothes, forcing herself to keep seated so her feet wouldn't hurt, although she wished more than anything to be able to swim circles around the room. "But—she was no longer there?"

"He said they departed a few weeks ago for the Diels— mountain country, which is apparently where Lord Carlo is from—to be married."

"Who is this Lord Carlo?" This was sounding worse all the time. "Dosia only mentioned boys."

"Maybe Lord Carlo is a boy," Swift said. "I heard about a baby king one time."

Or maybe Lord Carlo had heard about Dosia somehow, or seen her from a window, and decided to claim her, Esmerine thought.

Esmerine had come so far already. The more she learned of Dosia's fate, the more she felt as if a piece of her own self had broken off and fallen into the ocean. But how could she follow Dosia to the Diels?

"Are you . . . all right?" Alan asked.

She nodded wordlessly. Panic made her flush. The room was unbearably stuffy.

"Does Dosia still remember how to read?" he asked.

"Only a little . . ." Alan had taught them both some letters, but she felt certain Dosia had forgotten.

"Maybe you could get a letter to her."

"Maybe," she whispered, her voice cracking. She swallowed, thinking of the boys who had been killed in the ship's graveyard when she was young, and the shock and grief their mothers had experienced. Sometimes terrible things happened and there was nothing one could do, but she had never thought it could happen to her family. And Dosia wasn't even dead. Esmerine didn't want Dosia to be dead, but if she was miserable and Esmerine would never see her again, it was almost worse.

Was it awful to think so?

Why did Dosia have to go after humans in the first place? Esmerine had *warned* her. She still went. Why did she have to be so stupid, so stubborn?

"The Diels . . . ," Alan said. "I could be there and back again in four days . . . Might take me another day or two to find her, but I have no doubt that if I ask after her, I'll find her quickly enough . . ."

Esmerine knew it was too much to ask—a week of travel, for a girl he barely seemed to remember, just to tell Esmerine if she was all right. And if she wasn't all right, Esmerine's heart would scarcely be eased.

"I could go," Swift said. "You could spare me for a week."

"Have you ever been to the Diels before?" Alan asked.

"No, but they're just north, right? It can't be that hard. We have maps around here, and I've been as far as Torna. I can ask at the messenger post there."

"I don't know," Alan said. "You're rather young to be going that far by yourself. What if you run into trouble?"

"What do you think I did to make money before you came along?" Swift said. "I used to steal hats sometimes when I couldn't find better work. That was as dangerous as anything. I can take a beating. I doubt the Diels will give me worse than that. Anyway, you were a messenger last year and you're only a few years older than me."

Swift was not so young as Tormy after all, then; he was just small for his age. Even so, Esmerine felt a pang of guilt. "I can't ask you to go all that way for my sister. You don't even know her."

"Fandarsee are supposed to see the world," Swift said. "And you've come a long way looking for her. I *want* to do it."

"I suppose it's up to Belawyn, in any case," Alan said dismissively.

"Think about what message you want me to bring your sister," Swift said, but all Esmerine could think about just then was that she'd be spending at least a week in the human world, and all for just one exchange of a message.

Chapter Eight

I don't have any place to stay," Esmerine said with some reluctance. She didn't want to rely on Alan's charity when he didn't seem to bear even the slightest feeling toward her anymore. "If I sold this statue, would it be enough for an inn?"

"There's a spare room upstairs," Alan said. "You can stay. It's only a week."

She barely had a chance to thank him before a young man came in looking for political tracts, and Alan was more than happy to attend him.

Esmerine flipped through the history book, although it was difficult to truly read when she was so distracted by her clothing. Her stays and tight sleeves held her shoulders back, and she couldn't bend her elbows much, forcing her to hold the book in her lap. The stays were cutting into the sides of her stomach, and she was beginning to feel sore there. Dosia had been dressing like this for weeks now—almost two turns of the moon. How could she bear it? The more Esmerine thought of it, the more she itched and ached and fidgeted, and she just wanted to draw one deep breath. She hooked her finger beneath the stays and tried to pull them away to get some air, but not only was it impossible, her breast almost popped free. Flushing, she glanced Alan's way but he was still talking to the customer, and Swift had slipped out the back.

She stood to stretch, but her feet immediately ached with pain that vanished as soon as she sat down again. Human clothes were so sweaty and constricting! Panic crept over her. She slipped her feet out of her shoes, but the stockings were still itchy, and she could feel the tight ribbons above her knees holding them in place. How she wanted to tear those ribbons free! She could at least take off the bonnet, although she could hardly lift her arms with the tight sleeves she wore.

"I was just discussing this with another customer; most of us agree that you can't just let the people have free rein over the government, and yet . . ." Alan and the man were droning on with some discussion. She tried to listen, but her mind rebelled.

Heat spread through her chest, and her tongue was dry, her heart beating faster. She was feeling a little dizzy. She stood up and tried to walk to the door for some fresh air, but funny lights appeared inside her head, and suddenly darkness blanked her vision. She slumped, and although she didn't quite lose consciousness, she felt disoriented and couldn't see.

"Whoa," Alan said, and in another moment he had her arm and was helping her up. "When did you last eat or drink, Esmerine?"

"I don't know . . ." Her head was still black and spinning.

"I'll come back tomorrow," the other man said. "I hope you feel much better, miss."

"I'm sorry," Esmerine said, close to tears. "I didn't think I'd faint . . . I just—I've never been so hot and my clothes are so tight and—I've been so much trouble—" Nothing was going as she'd planned.

"It's all right. It's very different here." Still holding her arm, Alan locked the shop door. "Can you make it up the stairs?"

Her vision was starting to clear a little, but her heart was still pounding, and her feet stung, and she wanted to sob at the thought of stairs, but she said, "Yes." She'd already done a good job humiliating herself around him.

The narrow stairs made slow groaning noises when stepped on. Somehow or another she managed to make it upstairs and into the spare room.

"Lie down," Alan said. "I'll get you some water." He opened the window.

Once she was on the bed, with a sea-scented breeze blowing across her, Esmerine began to calm a little. Despite the street noise, the room was airy and peaceful, and very much Alan's taste. A bookshelf faced her from one wall, and on the other, a large desk with an angled top and stool, obviously meant to accomodate a Fandarsee's wings.

Just then, Alan returned with a cup of water and a bowl of berries.

"You'll feel better with something to eat and drink," he said, sitting on the edge of the bed. He regarded her a moment and then offered her his wing so she could pull herself upright. His skin was warmer than hers, but dry against her sweaty palms.

"I'm sorry," she said again. "I don't know what came over me. I don't usually *faint*. Even when I haven't eaten." She sucked down the cup of water he gave her and immediately started hiccuping. Every convulsion made her ribs ache. Just when she was starting to recover, Alan got to see her *hiccuping*. She desperately wanted out of the stays.

"Esmerine, listen. You just got here. You're not used to being stuffed into human clothes or being out in the heat and the dry air—sitting on rocks or beaches isn't the same as going into the city. It's perfectly understandable, and if you're going to be here for a week, this won't be the last of your miseries, I'm sure. Swift will go after Dosia, and you try and rest. I'm going to send Ginnia in here to help you out of your clothes."

He left the room. She wished he wouldn't go, until she reminded herself that he was only being nice because she'd nearly collapsed in his bookstore.

Ginnia was clearly the hired help, a girl in an apron with

very kind eyes set in a round face that was homely but entirely likable.

"No wonder you're so miserable, miss. This dress is meant for somebody smaller."

"But I don't have any other."

"Rest for now. Maybe you can get something in the market."

"I don't have any money."

"I'm sure Master Dare will know what to do." Ginnia took her empty water cup.

"I didn't come here to trouble him," Esmerine insisted, but Ginnia was heading for the door and didn't respond. Esmerine heard her murmuring to Alan in another room. She heard him say testily, "I can't just—" The rest was lost, but it was obviously about her.

The worst part was that she couldn't simply leave and deny his help. She *did* need his help. Now that she was here, she wished she had never found him again. Her memories of him were so much better, and now they would be tarnished.

She ate the berries and drifted off to sleep. The house had gone quiet. She woke some time later when Alan entered carrying a sky-blue dress with a cream-colored bodice. "Maybe this will fit you better?"

"Alan, really—I don't want you to go to any trouble on my account."

"Nonsense," he said. "No one is holding a knife to my throat. This wasn't any trouble, and it's out of fashion. I think you're courageous to come so far looking for your sister. Foolish, maybe, but courageous."

"Well, I *know* it's a little foolish," she said, irked.

He paused. "I heard my father was here."

"Oh yes. I'm so sorry I forgot to tell you."

"You spoke to him?"

"It was after you'd gone. And then Swift came in while he was here."

"Did you tell him who you were?"

"No. I remembered you telling me a while ago that he wouldn't be happy if he knew we were friends."

He smiled weakly. "That's good."

"Would he be upset that we talked even?"

"Oh, he's just—" Alan shook his head. "Fandarsee are supposedly so worldly and open minded, but it's not true."

"So he doesn't approve of mermaids?"

Alan shook his head. "He doesn't approve of anything out of step with our family's reputation. He'd rather I was furthering my education back home, but he sees no point in the things I'm interested in, philosophy and such. He's always asking me what it's supposed to do for anyone. My family has been of a scientific bent, generally. One of my great-uncles discovered bacteria, and I told you how my grandfather discovered a planet. I guess he won't be happy until I discover something."

Esmerine didn't know what bacteria even was. Maybe some kind of medicine? "That doesn't seem very fair! What if there aren't any more planets to discover?"

"Oh, I'm sure there's something, I'm just not interested in planets and bacteria the way I am in . . . other things, like how people think, or what they believe. I don't know why." He ran his fingers through his hair and looked to the window. The light was lower and cooler now, as even long summer days must come to an end. "Ah, well. It doesn't matter. He won't come around again too soon. He hates Sormesen. You just rest, and we'll have dinner in an hour or two. I'll send Ginnia to help you dress."

"I should write that letter to my sister for Swift," she said.

"Later," he said. "I'll show you how to write with quill and ink and paper."

One thing she had forgotten about Alan was how confusing he could be—irritable one moment, kind the next. Now, instead of resting properly, she found herself thinking of how he would arrive on the island, and she would suggest a story to act out, and he would protest and make excuses until she coaxed him into it. She remembered telling Dosia it was as if he thought he'd get in trouble if he had any fun, although no Fandarsee were around to witness him playing. Even other merfolk rarely took an interest in their island, which had no olive trees or other foods to entice gatherers.

"Well, it must be awful to be a winged person," Dosia had said. "The way he's always talking about school. I think he's too serious."

"But he can fly. That must make up for a lot."

Dosia rolled her eyes. "But he can't swim. So we're even."

Dosia was practical that way. She might desire things that

were difficult to obtain, like seeing the surface world, but she never desired impossible things, like flying. And she never seemed to envy anyone.

The thought started creeping back in, that Esmerine might never see Dosia again, and she shoved it down before it could fully flower. She needed her wits about her and her emotions safely buried, at least until she was back home again.

Chapter Nine

Ginnia returned before long to help Esmerine dress for dinner. She didn't lace her stays as tightly, but Esmerine still hated the feel of the rigid ribs and sturdy cloth hugging her chest. The sky-blue dress had loose sleeves that afforded far more movement, but she was used to her bare skin moving through soft water. She would never get used to the short breaths and the hem of a skirt getting underfoot.

"Do I need to wear the shoes in the house?" she asked Ginnia, whose look of amusement was answer enough.

"No sense wearing out those stockings." Ginnia led Esmerine from the dim bedroom. Dusk had crept up almost unnoticed until Esmerine came into a dining room lit by a candle and glowing hearth fire. Sometimes the mermen started a fire on the islands for some purpose or another, but only certain men knew how, and children couldn't come near, so Esmerine had never been close enough to fire to feel the heat. An older woman with gray curls spilling sideways from a squarish black cap was sitting quite near it, smoking a pipe. Could this be Belawyn? Esmerine couldn't believe a mermaid would smoke.

Ginnia went to stir the pot while Swift waved Esmerine to an empty seat. Alan was pouring something red into a glass. "Esmerine, do you want wine or water?" he asked.

"I've never tasted wine."

He poured a little in a cup and handed it to her. She took a sip. It was not at all sweet or salty, just nasty and like nothing else she had ever tasted.

Swift laughed. "She doesn't like it."

"It's an acquired taste," the older woman said, giving Esmerine a sly smile. Her lips were thin and painted, and her eyes had a combination of squint and slant as if she were looking very keenly at everything. "So, Alan tells me you're Esmerine. I'm Belawyn. I own the shop."

"And you're . . . a mermaid?"

"That's right, my pearl."

"A siren?"

"Not a siren. Just one of the common folk."

"How did you end up here?"

"Well, the shop belonged to a former husband. We were only

married a year before I guess he'd had enough of me and departed this mortal coil, leaving me with the shop. I've never been much for books, but one must eat somehow."

"I mean . . . why did you leave the sea?"

"Oh—" Belawyn sipped her wine. "There's no written rule that you have to be a poor fool of a siren to see the world."

"None of our rules are written," Esmerine said.

"Good thing," Belawyn said. "They make enough trouble without being on paper."

Esmerine had never seen an old person complain about rules so much. Most of the old women she knew were the ones who enforced the rules. "Do you live above the shop too?" she asked.

"I live in a cottage not far from here," Belawyn said. "Alan rents these rooms for a song, which suits me fine. I never was too fond of this place. It's drafty all winter, the roof leaks, and there's no room for a garden."

The heat from the hearth warmed Esmerine's left side, and on the right, a breeze drifted through the windows. The air had cooled with the darkness. Esmerine wondered how her mother and father were doing without her. Night was a quiet time beneath the sea. Was her mother lying awake wondering if Esmerine was all right? She wished she had a way to tell them what she had learned.

Alan gave Esmerine a cup of water and sat beside her.

"So, Swift was saying your charming father paid us a visit today?" Belawyn said.

"Oh, we don't need to talk about that." Alan sipped his wine. "Swift, could you not hoard the butter?"

Alan's servant girl circled the table, filling bowls with fish stew. The fish smelled fishier than Esmerine was used to, and steam rose from it. Esmerine had never eaten hot food before. "Just a little, please," she whispered, unsure if she would like it.

"We ought to talk about your father. I'm starting to regret ever accepting money from you. If I'd known it was really from him, and that he would hover around every week, I wouldn't have taken it. It's making me quite uncomfortable. I could sell the place, but I hate to become one of those old women who sits in the house all day, with a portrait of myself in my glory days staring down at me."

"Why not sell your portrait?" Swift offered. "You used to be a looker, or else the artist was being nice; I bet someone would buy it."

Belawyn smacked his shoulder with the back of her hand.

Alan frowned. "If this place shuts down, I'll have to go home."

"Well, Alan, dear, I hate to be honest—it just isn't my style— but part of the problem might be the way you keep thrusting books at people that they don't even understand, and curling your lip when they want something amusing, or, dare I say, tit-illating."

"It isn't my fault if everyone wants to read a bunch of non-sense! You have travelers from all over the world coming through

Sormesen, stopping in this shop. There's a real opportunity to sell them something of *value*."

"Is that your father talking, or you?" Belawyn arched a nearly nonexistent brow.

"My father does not talk *through* me. But why should we waste our time selling trash?"

"So you'd like to control and censor what people read, then?"

"Well—no! No, not that," Alan said. "I just . . ."

"Alan—" Esmerine didn't want to thrust herself in the middle of an argument that had obviously been brewing for some time, and she doubted she could save the shop, but she might be able to repay Alan and Swift. "Since Swift will be gone for the week, maybe I could stand outside with those . . . Hauzdeen pamphlets and try to sell them. I could sing about them, and people would want to buy them then."

"Esmerine—you're a siren too?" Alan began. "I thought only Dosia—"

"Yes, I'm a siren too." She couldn't tell if he was upset by this or only surprised. And why should he be either?

"So you're saying you would *hoodwink* them into buying Hauzdeen?" Alan asked.

Belawyn cackled. "It's the only way we're going to sell all those copies! Why, if I could sing customers into buying twenty-volume encyclopedias, I would!"

"It's not hoodwinking!" Esmerine said, chagrined. "Siren

magic doesn't work if they don't have *some* interest in it to begin with. Although . . . I don't know why you can't sell plenty of books, Alan. You used to bring me the most wonderful books. All those stories about princesses and winged travelers and trees that turned into people and people that turned into animals . . ."

Alan's ears flushed. "Well—you will only be here a week, until Swift returns from the Diels. I hardly think it's enough time to save us from our troubles."

"But it couldn't hurt," Belawyn said. "And it could help. It could help a great deal."

Alan frowned into his soup, poking apart the flesh of a white fish with his spoon, and didn't respond.

Chapter Ten

When Belawyn stood to go, she reached for a cane propped against the back of her chair and limped to the stairs. She wiggled a beckoning finger to Esmerine.

"You ought to use a little of that siren song on Alan, my pearl. The boy needs to loosen his cravat."

Alan was still sitting at the table, and while Esmerine didn't think he couldn't hear them, he stared at them over his cup and took a slow sip.

"Siren song has never had any effect on him. At least, not when he was a kid."

"Well, doesn't that just figure." Belawyn patted her shoulder. "Good luck."

Esmerine couldn't tell to what degree Belawyn was teasing.

"You should head home, Bel," Alan said. "Swift needs sleep if he's going to the Diels tomorrow morning."

Swift was waiting to walk Belawyn home.

"Trying to run me out of my own building, eh? Behave yourselves, you two," Belawyn said, which made Alan's ears turn red again. As soon as she disappeared down the stairwell, he turned to Ginnia.

"Ginnia, if you could help Esmerine to bed before anything else, I'd be obliged."

"Yes, sir."

He departed the room without even saying good night.

Ginnia put a hand on Esmerine's shoulders, guiding her into the bedroom. "Don't mind him. He gets awfully moody when his father comes around, and Belawyn enjoys goading him."

Ginnia helped Esmerine out of the dress and stays and showed her the chamber pot. Esmerine frowned. The human world was so dirty. Under the ocean, holes in the rocks channeled currents through privy rooms to whisk waste into the deep sea; it didn't just sit there and reek.

Ginnia had pulled back the covers for her. She slipped her feet beneath them and pulled the blanket over her shoulder. She knew that was the intention with human blankets, but the weight didn't feel right. She folded it back to her waist. A feather sneaked out from the pillow to prick her cheeks. Her chemise clung to her sticky skin. She tried to think of something else. Her ear began following unfamiliar sounds—voices down the street somewhere, and a continual creak. What was that? Something outside? She looked out the window to search out the source. It was the wooden bookstore sign, swaying in the wind.

Esmerine had a wild urge to tear out of bed and run home, where familiar waters would welcome her back to a safe embrace. Alan didn't want her here. She had been such a fool to seek out a boy who had once taught her to read but didn't care for her at all.

She shoved off the covers. She was drowning in fabric. The air was too hot, and her body too heavy. She yanked off her chemise and threw it aside, but it felt strange to be naked with legs. The legs were a part of her, but as she stared at them in the moonlight, they seemed alien limbs, like her tail had been torn apart and stripped of scales and the legs were all that remained. There were bruises at her waist where the stays had been too tight, and dirt between her toes.

She wanted her tail and she wanted her mother. When she closed her eyes, she could almost feel her mother's arms around her, her shell necklace against Esmerine's skin, and her firm touch on the back of Esmerine's head.

Home felt so far away, but she kept telling herself it was only a day's travel. Her parents were sleeping soundly in the bay. She could go home soon. She wasn't trapped here. Not like Dosia, she reminded herself.

She tossed and turned all night, but finally the sun came

through the curtains and she heard movement in the kitchen. She wished she could float out of bed with a flick of her tail. Waking up here seemed such an exhausting prospect.

She couldn't lace her stays herself, so she emerged in her chemise. Alan was at the table with a cup of black liquid and a paper in hand. He glanced up at her very briefly. "Oh—Ginnia, our guest is awake; could you . . . ?"

"Of course, sir," she replied, shaking her head at him behind his back, smiling at Esmerine.

"Is there some way to wash?" Esmerine asked as Ginnia laced the stays over a fresh chemise, while Esmerine's body still had all the grime of the past day.

"Wash what?"

"Myself?"

"You'll only be here a week," Ginnia said. "Why do you need to wash? Maybe Belawyn has some scent you can borrow, if you'd like."

"No, it's all right." Esmerine wanted sand and salt water to scrub with, not *scent*.

"Anyway, you look lovely. Would you like any coffee? Soup?" Ginnia led her back into the kitchen. "I apologize that we don't have any porridge. Master Dare prefers a light breakfast."

"Soup is fine," Esmerine said. As if she knew a thing about breakfasts here to begin with.

"She might rather have water than coffee," Alan said, still looking at his paper.

"I do, actually."

Ginnia brought the cup of water and a bowl of soup to the opposite end of the table. Alan turned a page. Esmerine slurped the soup, surprised to find such familiar food—strands of seaweed floated in the pale broth. He obviously didn't gather seaweed on her islands anymore but he still got it somewhere.

She felt Alan's eyes on her, but when she looked up to catch them, he was back to the paper.

"What are you reading?" she asked.

"Just the newspaper."

"Oh." She had to resist touching the pages. "Could you read any to me? Like you used to, with the stories?"

He hesitated, tugging at his necktie, and then shifted to sit next to her, rather than across, so she could see the words while he read to her. She bent her head over the newspaper, twisting her hair and pulling it around her neck so it wouldn't fall on the pages.

"You know what?" he said. "I don't know if this paper is the thing." He stood. "I'll be right back."

He returned with a little red book she recognized.

"*Tales of Many Lands*," she exclaimed, reaching out to touch the dear cover, with its worn edges.

"I haven't opened this book in many years," Alan said. "Not since the last time I saw you. I always wanted to give it to you, but I knew it would only disintegrate under the sea."

"Let me see . . ."

She had always loved the pictures. The book fell open

naturally to her favorite story, "The Girl Who Loved a Bird." There was a picture of the girl transforming into a bird on the last page. After three trials, with the bird's help, she could join him.

"You always loved this one best," he said.

"I guess I wanted to fly."

"Do you . . . still?" He looked away from her, seeming uncomfortable.

"I guess I want a lot of things," she said. "But I'll work on the ones that seem possible first." *Possible . . . and safe.*

"Like what?" he asked. His eyes traveled back to her. She remembered his eyes as brown, but now she noticed they were only brown at the edges, bleeding into a mossy green. It was the first really good look at him she'd had since arriving, and for a moment—perhaps it was the appearance of the old familiar book—she was overwhelmed with memories of him. When she'd first seen him all grown up, she had thought him strange, but now that was already fading. He actually looked the same, just a little older, only she'd forgotten all the subtleties of him, like the color of his eyes and the straight, firm lines of his nose and mouth that seemed to match the long, swift lines of his wings. Everything about him seemed sharper and faster than a merman.

"Your hair used to be longer," she said.

He didn't seem bothered that she hadn't answered his question. "Well, it got in my eyes in the wind. And you always wore yours in a braid."

"It gets tangled underwater, so my mother would braid it in the morning. When I was little, I mean. My mother doesn't braid my hair anymore. Of course." Her cheeks heated. "The sirens, we keep ourselves busy while we're waiting for ships by combing our hair."

"That sounds very scintillating."

"Well, we don't just comb our hair. We sing and tell stories."

"No, I know." He shook his head slightly. "The merfolk sing beautifully. Like the sea itself. I had a hard time sleeping when I became a messenger and traveled away from the ocean." He paused. "Do you miss—that is, I always felt terrible for leaving when I was your only source of books."

"It's—it's all right . . . Everyone back home thinks I'm very odd for missing them, anyway." She flipped the pages of *Tales of Many Lands*. The fact that the book would disintegrate underwater like the books in shipwrecks burned in her heart like her feet burned when they touched the ground. If Alan could admit to missing the sound of the sea, she could admit to missing books. "I suppose . . . I just want to know things. I'm not always sure why. I thought I wanted to be a siren, I thought I would be happy then, but I wasn't. I was so angry at Dosia for leaving, but I also . . ." She trailed off. It was so hard to explain the raw desire she felt for something that was unnameable, something that had no purpose for a mermaid. Was it enough to want to know something just to know it?

"She gave you an excuse to come here, didn't she?" Alan said.

"Of course not! I would never have come if it weren't for her. I already worry what the other sirens must think of me."

"I'm surprised that you became a siren," he said. "With Dosia, I'm not surprised, but you . . ."

"Why wouldn't I be a siren?"

"Aren't sirens always drawn to human men? Isn't it what makes siren magic so potent to them? I just never thought you were drawn to human men."

"Well, I'm *not*."

"Well, what are you drawn to?"

Her stomach fluttered. "I guess—it must be—books." True. Just not entirely true. Other mermaids were content to marry mermen and giggle about humans. Why did she have to be so drawn to dark, clever eyes and graceful wings and childhood memories that wouldn't leave her alone? "It's your fault," she added.

"I know. I—I don't know why I taught you to read when you can't have any books."

"I'm not sorry," she said. She let the book fall open once again to that girl transforming into a little black shape taking flight, swift and free. Everything about it pierced her. The way the book felt in her hands, delicate and precious with its textured cover and slightly browned pages. The way the words ran across the page in perfect lines, expressing order and permanence. And of course the picture, reaching into her soul and twisting, whispering of things she could not have.

Alan put his thumbs on the edge of the book just above hers

and gently shut it. "Maybe I should give you a tour of the bookstore since you'll be helping Belawyn out this week."

"Yes. Please."

Once she finished her soup, she followed him downstairs. The bookstore front faced the morning sun, and the beams slanted in and fell on the shelves, like the sky was pointing a benevolent finger at them.

"Those are novels on the back shelves," Alan said. "With plays and poetry beside them. On the left we have books of philosophy, science, botany, and medicine. On the right, political tracts, history, and travel, including guidebooks for Sormesen, which are very popular."

"Where are the books like this?" She held up *Tales of Many Lands*. "The books you used to bring me?"

"That would be with the fairy tales and myths, which are by poetry. Other books we used to read are peppered all through here—some history, some narratives, some novels . . . but, of course, those aren't the books I'm trying to sell."

"Why not?"

"Because . . . Fandarsee have a certain responsibility to educate. People look to us for ideas, not fanciful things. I might not be discovering a planet, but I hope I assist people in discovering ideas that might lead to more ideas, and so on."

"Ideas about what?"

"Well, anything important. Like the book I'm reading. It's about whether people have inherent moral values. What is right and wrong. That's quite important."

"I suppose, but don't myths teach that too?"

"Maybe, but it isn't the sort of thing learned men discuss."

Another thing that hadn't really changed about Alan was that sometimes she didn't understand him at all. "Why not? Isn't it interesting?"

"It is, but you don't understand. It's not . . . *important*."

"No, you're right, I don't understand. I guess I'm glad I'm not a 'learned man.'"

He looked briefly affronted, but then he either realized how silly he sounded or he simply gave up on her, she wasn't sure which. "Anyway, you've seen the bookstore," he said. "Now, I ought to show you how to write with a quill so we can send Swift off with that letter for Dosia."

They returned to the desk in her bedroom. He jerked open a drawer and took a few sheets of paper from the stack inside. "You've only ever written with a stick and sand, correct? Pen and ink is a bit different."

He showed her how to mix ink from powder and dip her quill into the pot.

"I already have these few ready," he said, gesturing to the waiting quills, their fronds trimmed to mere puffs at the ends. "But later I'll show you how to trim the tip. Let me know if you have trouble."

"All right."

He left her alone, and she carefully wrote *Dear Dosia*. She remembered that letters were always addressed that way in books, and was quite proud of herself for beginning a proper human letter with a real quill.

After that, it became more difficult. *What happened to you?* she wrote. *Are you all right?* From there, she hardly knew what else to say. That felt like all that really mattered at the moment.

She didn't realize how long she'd been there until Swift appeared in the doorway, munching on bread, hair mussed from sleep. "Is the letter ready?"

"Um . . . almost."

He peered at her paper. "Do you need help?"

"No—well—I can write, but—"

"That doesn't look like much of a letter," Swift said.

"I know it's not!" She sighed. "I have no idea what to say. This might be the last time I ever get to communicate with her . . ." She bit her lip, as if it might loosen the constriction in her throat.

"Why don't you add that you miss her and—I don't know—you hope she's happy?"

"Well, sure, but—that sounds so feeble. And I'm so afraid I'll make things worse. I don't want her to cry."

"Does she cry a lot?"

"She doesn't cry a *lot*, but she might cry from my letter no matter what I say. I'm afraid I'll cry trying to write it."

Swift frowned. "I don't know. I don't have family. But if she's going to cry no matter what, you might as well write what you think."

"I guess you're right."

He left, and she wrote as quickly as she could—each letter had to be formed carefully. *I miss you so much. If there was anything I could do to save you, I would. Every day and night I wish you hadn't gone back to see those humans, but since there is no undoing it, I just hope you find some happiness. However far away we might be for the rest of our lives, we'll always be sisters, and I'll think of you every day . . . I have to end this letter now so I can send it along. I'm afraid I'm about to cry horribly . . .*

She folded the letter and pressed it to her chest, as if it could stem the bleeding of her heart.

Chapter Eleven

She brought the letter downstairs, tucked between the pages of *Tales of Many Lands*.

"I'll be back soon, and tell you everything," Swift said, before he spread his wings and flew away. She watched him vanish from sight, which didn't take long, as three- and four-story buildings blocked her view of the broad sky.

"Excuse me, miss."

Esmerine turned to see a pretty young girl wearing a wide-brimmed straw hat trimmed with an excess of flowers. Her dress was equally fussy, made of glossy peach-colored fabric with ivory ribbons. An older woman, in a plain dress, followed her and carried a parcel—a chaperone, Esmerine guessed.

"I'm looking for a book. Something that won't bore me to death. What book do you have there?"

"*Tales of Many Lands*?" Esmerine kept it clutched to her chest.

"Is it any good?"

"I like it," she said hesitantly.

"How much?" The girl motioned for the older woman to step forward and presumably produce money.

"Oh no—this one's not for sale. Maybe there's another copy." Esmerine opened the door. The girl followed, almost stepping on Esmerine, as if impatient with her pace.

"We aren't open yet," Alan said. He was standing on a stool, arranging a few books on the shelf, and didn't even look over.

"You're all here," the girl said. "Why wouldn't you be open? I want *Tales of Many Lands*."

"We don't have it," Alan said, still fussing with the shelves.

"Then I want the one she's holding." The girl motioned for the older woman again. Coins were brought out. Alan finally stepped down.

"It's not for sale," he said. "That's a personal copy."

"Well, you shouldn't have books on display that aren't for sale."

"You don't want that book anyway," Alan said. "You probably want some tripe like *A Courtesan and a Gentleman*, like girls always want. It's no wonder humans think women can't handle education. My God, they don't teach them a thing about proper—"

"Do you know who I am?" the girl interrupted. "I am the daughter of Lord Elbasio, and—"

"I don't really care who you're the daughter of, particularly not if you're going to make such rude demands—"

"*I* make rude demands? When my father hears about this—"

Esmerine watched all this with horrified fascination. Despite a certain satisfaction in watching Alan yell at the girl, who had been less than polite about obtaining Esmerine's book without even caring what it was—it was no way to sell anything.

"I think there's been a misunderstanding," Esmerine said. "This book, you see, it's really for children. I just happened to be holding it to show some children I know who'll be stopping by later. But if you want something that isn't boring— Alan, do you remember that book about that man who goes to this island colony, and he doesn't mean to stay, but there's a girl there, and that part with the fire? And she has a pet monkey, I think?"

"You mean *Penelope's Island*? We do have that."

"I've heard of it," the girl said, still looking peeved at Alan. "Is it any good?"

"Yes, it's wonderful. Oh, there's this part I always loved where he first comes to the island, and she has this little house, and she invites him in and they have tea—I've never had tea, but it sounded like the most delightful thing to have, and the way everything is described is so fascinating. There's that one, and there's another one that is very good about this family who works on a farm in some other country where it's cold—"

"That would be *A Measure of Prosperity*," Alan said.

"It's sad in a few parts, but it makes the happier parts better. The characters in that one are just so real, even though I didn't know anything about snow or farms, I just liked them all so much. Alan, do we have two copies of them? I want to read them again just thinking about it. I can hardly remember the best parts anymore!" Esmerine had almost forgotten she was talking to anyone, remembering the stories Alan had read her while she sat beside him and followed the words and how she had cried when the father died. It had been so long since she'd read them, it would be almost as good as the first time, if she could even see them and hold them—

"Well, I suppose those do sound good," the girl said. "I'll take a copy of each."

Alan took her money, and she left with the only copies of the novels. Esmerine never even had a chance to look at them.

On the other hand, she had sold two books without even a hint of hoodwinking. She turned to Alan. "Don't you think you were a little rude to that girl?"

"She was being ridiculous. Books on *display*? It wasn't on display, you were holding it, and I don't care if her father is the Lord of the Dead—"

"She was just some rich girl who wanted to buy any old thing that wasn't boring. You didn't even try. Don't you want to pay off your debts to your father?"

"She bought the books," he said, "because you sounded so passionate about them."

Just then, Belawyn came hobbling in the door. "Good morning, my pearl. Ready to do some hoodwinking?"

"I suppose so," Esmerine said.

"Well, obviously we won't send you out to hawk in the square like Swift. You can just sit outside and sing your little siren heart out. Alan, carry a chair out front for the lady, would you?"

It was well known that siren magic was more effective on some humans than others, but it was fairly effective on everyone. It did feel like hoodwinking when, within moments, two fair-haired men with packs on their backs halted their marching, folded their maps, and watched her. When she finished singing, they applauded, and when she motioned them into the shop, they went. They came out some time later with parcels.

Shade was nonexistent, and once she began to feel hot, she started noticing all the other little discomforts. She nudged her feet out of her shoes. Proper or not, no one would notice under her skirts.

Before the sun rose too high, Belawyn brought her in and sent her upstairs for a drink of water and some bread and cheese. When Esmerine finished lunch, Belawyn said, "We've already sold as much in a morning as we usually do in a day."

"Do you think they *like* the books?"

"When they hear your music, they seem to want something beautiful," Belawyn said. "Make of that what you will."

Esmerine smiled.

"If you'd care to rest your voice, I could use some help inside the shop. I'm sending Alan off with some deliveries."

"Of course." Esmerine was glad to stay inside out of the hot sun. Belawyn was sitting at the counter, smoking her pipe. The one customer currently in the shop, a broad-chested man in a bright-green coat, seemed content to browse alone. Alan donned his hat, tipped it at Esmerine in an automatic way, and left with a parcel.

"Sit with me, my pearl. I want to know a little more about you."

Esmerine sat, a bit apprehensively.

"So, tell me. You came looking for your lost siren sister, is that right?"

"Of course." Belawyn already knew this.

"And in a week's time, Swift will return with news, and you will return to your family in reasonable contentment, besides, of course, some lingering regret over your sister."

"I'll never be content . . ."

"Do you know, most of the time when sirens leave the sea, their family doesn't chase after them at all?"

"I know. But most merfolk, of course, don't know how to walk, so coming after a siren may not be an option. My sister and I used to play with Alan on the islands out in the bay. Alan couldn't go underwater so we had to go to him. We walked a lot."

"I must say, I'm trying to imagine Alan playing with mermaids on an island, and I can't, but of course I believe you. Still, I think you must have sacrificed a lot, and pushed aside all the stories of human cruelty you have ever heard, to come here looking for a sister you know you can't save."

Esmerine shrugged one shoulder. "She's my sister. I had to try. Why did *you* come here?"

"I swallowed the lies I was told for a long time," Belawyn said. "I was told how humans were dirty and stupid and cruel, down to the last teat-sucking babe. But I was secretly fascinated by human ships and buildings, though it was shameful to say so aloud. My mother thought I'd be chosen as a siren, but when they asked me, I refused."

"You refused becoming a siren?" Esmerine had never heard of anyone refusing such an exalted position.

"I didn't want to spend my life sitting on rocks, hoping some fisherman would steal me away when what I really wanted wasn't a fisherman, or any man, but simply a different life. So I apprenticed to the village healer instead. I thought I might find that more fulfilling."

"Didn't you?"

"No. I saw my life narrowing around me, as much a prison as any stolen siren. I kept sneaking away to the surface, to watch the human village in the distance. My father caught me trying to walk, and he was so furious that he threatened to lock a ring around the base of my tail so I couldn't change. But why do we have the ability to change into humans if none of us are ever meant to walk among them? I wondered that then, and I still do."

Esmerine had never wondered why. She had always simply accepted it, like she accepted the phases of the moon. It was fascinating to consider there might be a purpose. "Do you have any theories on why we can change?"

"I'm no philosopher," Belawyn said. "Don't want to be one either. I don't want to read theories about why people do this or that."

"I guess Alan is just curious about the world and he looks to books for answers. He's always been like that." Esmerine might argue with Alan, but she would still defend him to Belawyn.

"Now, when did I ever name names?" Belawyn grinned. "All I know is, the sea and the land have a relationship, and some of us feel it in our bones. Some of us want to be here, and there's no harm in it, if we're willing to make the sacrifice. Tell me what's the harm in living on our own terms? I'm my own woman, and a damned happy one. Don't ever bother with what people say about you."

"Well," Esmerine said. "That makes sense. But I don't want to stay here. My family misses me."

"I'm sure they do, but I wonder at your phrasing. Do they miss you, or do you miss them?"

"Of course I miss them too! I hardly need mention it." Esmerine's family wasn't like Belawyn's, that was certain. They would never forbid her from turning her tail to legs. "Are you the only mermaid in Sormesen?"

"Oh, besides a few stolen sirens, there are a handful of us, from different villages all along the coasts. They never talk about us back home, I imagine."

"I'd never heard of a mermaid leaving home who wasn't a siren."

"There are a few mermen too, although they have a harder

time with their feet. Humans are more likely to accept a lame woman than a man."

"But how do you ever get used to it? The clothes? The pain?"

"Just like you get used to anything," Belawyn said. "When you really want something."

Chapter Twelve

The next few days passed in what could have been a routine manner, except that nothing felt routine in the surface world. Every day brought new people from around the continent, with their varied clothes and accents and manners, and new foods. One day Alan came home from making deliveries with balls of dough drenched in honey and nuts. She had never tasted anything so sweet or so delicious, and she didn't tell him she had a stomachache all night. She never slept well anyway, so the discomfort seemed worth it.

In the morning, she sang for the shop, and in the afternoon, when Alan was usually out running errands, she watched Belawyn sell books in a languid way that drove her mad—if

Alan was too snobbish about his recommendations, Belawyn seemed more interested in gossip than bookselling. Esmerine suggested books when she could, for as days went by, she grew acquainted with some of the stock, especially books she remembered from her childhood. In the evening, she read the shop's contents. It was almost difficult to enjoy them, seeing so many at once and knowing she would never see them again at week's end. She held the memories close for when she was back under the sea.

Alan remained distant, even when they were alone with Ginnia at mealtimes. Sometimes Belawyn joined them for dinner, but not always. Usually Esmerine and Alan ate with their respective books open at their plates, but she had trouble concentrating. She would have rather talked to him, known how his life had been since their childhood.

Finally, one morning she decided to ask. "Alan, you said you used to be a messenger?"

"That's right," he said, still looking at the book. "Not for long."

"Why not?"

"I hated it."

"Why?"

Now he looked up. "Why the interest?"

"I just wondered what you'd been doing since I last knew you. How you ended up here. I mean, we used to be such good friends, it seems strange not to even talk when we have this week."

"Oh." He closed the book. Thank goodness. She had started

to hate whatever book he was reading. "It's not very interesting. Most Fandarsee go to the Academy and then become messengers for a time. We're supposed to see a bit of the world before we go on to further education or apprenticeships or so on."

"Why did you hate it? It seems travel would be interesting."

"Well, the messenger years are sort of the 'wild' years, your first time away from home and all. You're supposed to come back ready to settle down into adult life. I found the messenger culture distasteful, running around to different cities every day, drinking wine late into the night at the messenger posts . . ."

"That sounds fun, though. I mean, not the wine, I don't care for it. But you must meet lots of people."

"It's all very hollow," he said. "And somehow I was supposed to come back from *that* prepared to settle into a life of research and marriage like my father? If those were my wild years . . . well, they seemed wasted. So I quit and came to Sormesen, seeking some other fortune that suited me. I ended up here, where at least I can learn around books and different kinds of people, without all the running around and other nonsense."

"Oh." Esmerine thought it strange that he had left home to live with humans. It had been such a heavy decision for her to come just for a short while to help Dosia. Strange that he had done all this yet never come back to visit her. "Have you made a lot of friends here?"

"That isn't the point."

"What is the point?"

"Esmerine, my God but you ask a lot of questions."

"Well, I'm going to ask another one!" she said, her voice rising. "Why do you make me feel stupid for asking if you have friends or why you don't like fairy tales? Is your life only about books and studies and philosophies? When we used to play together, I looked forward to the books you brought and the things you told me, but we also used to have so much *fun*."

"We were children! I—I put those things aside when I went to the Academy. The whole world looks to us for knowledge. Maybe such frivolity is all right for merfolk because you don't have that reputation."

Esmerine made a face. He might not mean to insult her, but he still sounded superior. "Your people are very strange."

"*My* people are strange? What about how the other mermaids teased you because I brought you books? What about the fact that they didn't like you to take on a legged form? Seems to me they were afraid of what you might learn."

Esmerine had finished most of her soup, and couldn't eat more anyway. She pushed the bowl back. "They were trying to protect me from danger! Danger like what Dosia's gotten herself into."

"Danger? From me? A boy of ten with a book of fairy tales?"

"Well, they must've thought—" Yes, what *had* they thought? Why did they care if she learned to read? "I guess it was just that you were strange to them."

He made a frustrated sound. "So I had to leave that behind, didn't I?"

"What? Me?"

"You, and—what I'm trying to say is, it was time for me to grow up and concern myself with proper Fandarsee things, and for you to do the same. I suppose we learned from our friendship, but just as your world has no books, my world doesn't have the things your world has. Singing and dancing are for performers, and what you called 'theatricals' would be called 'children's games' where I'm from."

Esmerine regarded him fiercely. "How insulting you are! You enjoyed it at the time."

"I did!" he snapped. "But I couldn't keep coming to see you forever. You welcomed me, but the other merfolk looked at me with curiosity at best and quite often distaste."

"Well, they—I don't know—" She stopped, knowing it was true. Even four years after Alan left, she was commonly defined as the girl who played with the winged boy, with all that implied—the running around with legs, the writing on the sand. She had never been shunned, it was more of a mark—*Esmerine's a fine girl, very well behaved, but a bit odd*. In fact, she always felt she had to be well behaved, to prove herself. If they thought her odd, they did their best to ignore Alan's very existence. "I never realized you cared what they thought of you."

"I don't, but—" He stood, shaking his head slightly as he pushed in his chair. "We're just different, Esmerine."

She didn't quite agree, but she didn't argue either, because one thing was quite true—they were grown.

Chapter Thirteen

A few days can seem very long when full of new experience, but all the same, the end of the week came quickly. When Esmerine woke and Ginnia helped her into her stays and pinching shoes, she told herself that soon she would shed these things and feel water around her, recharge her magic and her soul. Her siren song grew weaker the longer she lived away from her element. At night especially she missed the water and her natural form so badly that she would wriggle and toss atop the blanket for hours without sleep.

When she sat with Alan at breakfast, it occurred to her that this might be their last breakfast together. It might be the last day she would see him. For all that he was nice to her some-times, likely he'd be relieved when she was gone.

That was fine. She might have had a bit of a romantic image of him in her head when she arrived, but the more time spent in his company, the more she wondered why she had ever built him up that way.

"Swift could be back any moment," he said, seeing the way she kept looking out the window.

"Yes. Oh, I hope the news about Dosia isn't too awful." Waiting for that was the hardest thing to bear.

"I suppose you'll leave as soon as he returns?"

"Well . . . yes, of course."

"Of course. Your family must be so anxious. But it's a shame in some ways. Tomorrow is a holy day, and the start of the sum-mer season. The bookshop will be closed. You could see a bit of the city. There's a reason people come here from all over the world, you know . . . we have some of the most famous monu-ments in all human creation."

"How would I see them, to begin with? I can't walk."

"Well, we've made such a nice profit this week—" He paused. "No, you're right. Even if we hired a carriage to get around, you would still want to see things up close. That wouldn't do."

"Oh, well," she said, but it was maddening to have come so far and be unable to tromp around the city like all the lucky tourists.

"Tonight is the children's procession," he said. "The churches all select children to sing and bear candles and walk the streets.

Some will come this way. At least . . . you could stay and watch that. A nice way to spend what could be your last night here."

"That would be nice."

"Are you still good at climbing trees?"

The question took her off guard. "I think so—why?"

"If we climb on the roof of my house, we can see the fireworks from the square at the closing of the procession."

"Oh—yes, I remember you telling me about fireworks. I'd love to see them." Esmerine wasn't so sure about climbing onto the roof of a two-story house, but she would figure that out later.

But there was no sign of Swift that day. It was too soon to worry, but Esmerine wondered what she'd do if he didn't turn up. How long could she wait? Besides, it seemed callous to leave. A part of her hoped for an excuse to have a few more days to read books in the shop and see the surface world, and another part of her despaired at the idea of remaining here much longer. The thought of leaving her dirty clothes behind and scrubbing herself in the sand was delicious to contemplate.

"Don't worry," Belawyn said when she bid Esmerine good night. "Swift will be back any day now. I trust the boy is as good at getting out of trouble as he is at getting into it."

After dinner, Alan and Esmerine went single file down the narrow alley to the back of the shop, where a solid old tree spread dark arms past the roof. The branches began just a foot from the ground. A perfect climbing tree, except that she had never climbed as high as a two-story house.

She kicked off her shoes and reached for a branch above her head while placing a foot on the lowest branch. The bark was unexpectedly rough on her toes. She sucked air through her teeth to avoid an exclamation of pain. Tree climbing had seemed easier when she was young. One would think her tolerance for pain would grow, but then again, it had never been so unrelenting . . .

The next branch was no better, although she masked it more easily. As much as she wanted to watch the fireworks from the roof, she was beginning to wonder if she could make it that far.

Suddenly Alan's fingers were on her waist. "Stop," he said. "Never mind. Come back down."

"But—" With a sigh, she let her feet drop to the ground again.

They stood in the deep-blue shadow of dusk, but his eyes picked up the gleam of a torch burning a few buildings down. He had that expression again, that pity she disliked.

He turned his back to her.

"Put your arms around my neck," he said, bending his knees a bit. "And hold on."

Her arms? Around his neck? Was he—*could* he—fly with her? She obeyed, grabbing the collar of his vest in her fists. In one motion, his legs straightened, his wings spread, and it seemed that he simply jumped onto the roof in one great impossible leap.

"Alan . . ." Esmerine slid slowly off his back. Her hands shook from even that brief, tantalizing flight. "I never knew you could do that!"

"I couldn't when we were kids," he said. "I wasn't that good at harnessing the wind. They don't teach Fandarsee kids to fly with a lot of weight until . . . well, around the time I stopped coming to see you." He scratched the back of his head.

"Oh, I wish you had been able to do it then! We would have had so much fun. Remember how you used to fly over the water and we'd grab your feet, and you'd pull us out and drop us?"

He gave a small laugh. "Of course! That was the best I could do back then."

The bookshop roof was only slightly sloped with irregularly shaped, flat stones for tiles rather than the more common reddish tiles. As a walking surface, it proved no more difficult than the steps and ruts of Sormesen's hilly roads. She settled herself near the point of the roof, bunching up her skirts for a little padding.

Alan crouched next to her. They faced the market square, a patchwork of roofs between the pillar where she had first seen Swift and the bookshop's roof. The night air was humid and carried a fragrance of flowers. Down the road, the procession of children bearing candles approached like a slow-moving tide. Their sweet song rose high and pure above the other noise of the city.

She could not yet make out faces, just the lights. In the warmth and song of the Sormesen night, she felt closer to Alan than she had since those days spent on their little island. She looked at him, and for a moment, he looked back. His eyes were warm in the sunlight, but at night they looked black and full of quiet intensity.

He started to say, "Maybe sometime I'll come and—" then stopped and shifted slightly away.

"What?"

"No, it's just—well, it is too bad I can't send a book home with you. But—you know. It's all right."

"Yes," she said quietly. He *could* visit her, she knew. She had seen his adult life now, and while it was busy, it wasn't so busy that he wouldn't have an occasional moment to fly to the islands and bring her a book. He had been about to suggest it, she was sure, but then what would the other sirens think if she was sitting on the rocks with them and suddenly Alan came flying by? People might have overlooked it when she was young, but she couldn't spend her adult life set apart from other merfolk because she liked books and befriended a Fandarsee. He understood that.

It felt like the last night of her childhood.

"Look," Alan said, as the procession drew near. "I'm not sure that boy is going to make it."

One child was slogging, arms drooping, candle wax dripping, eyes half closed. Esmerine and Alan both laughed gently. It was a strangely intimate sound on the quiet rooftop, and it made her shiver.

He put his wing around her, very lightly, fingers barely touching her shoulder. "A little cold?"

"A little," she lied. In truth, she felt like someone had started a fire in her core that was draining the heat from her fingers and toes, but leaving her warm within. Her heart was beating too fast. How could Alan make her feel this way? No merman had ever done this to her. What if this was the only time in her life she ever felt like this?

They both stared ahead, watching the slow march of the children and the soft glow of their candles. He left his wing around her, as if it were a casual gesture, but his body was stiff, and his toes clenched the edge of the roof tile.

Esmerine's back started to itch, and she didn't want to scratch it, in case he took the wing away. They sat very still for almost the entirety of the procession, moving only when they heard the slow flap of wings behind them.

Swift had returned. Alan jerked away from Esmerine, stood and stepped back, giving him room to land on the roof.

"What's going on?" Swift asked.

"Nothing," Alan said. "We're just watching the parade. Esmerine's cold up here. We should get her in the house, I suppose."

"Did you find my sister?" Esmerine said, already trying to read Swift's face for signs of the news.

"Yeah, I found her."

"And?" Esmerine wanted to shake Swift to get answers out of his mouth faster.

"Where do I begin? She lives in this huge house. She has her own quarters all to herself, and maids, and these little dogs with long hair that's always brushed, and this house . . . ! Why, if you spent one night there you could hardly bear to come back to this. It has statues and a fountain."

He continued, "And the food! I'd never seen so much meat, and it was full of spices and after that was this chocolate torte . . ."

"But . . . does she seem happy?"

"Well . . ."

Her shoulders slumped. "No? Swift, please tell me. Is she all right? I guess she's well fed, at least?"

"Well, I never actually saw *her* . . ."

Esmerine felt like her stomach had dropped through the roof. "What do you mean? Why not? Where was she?"

"Well, she was traveling with her husband. Visiting friends. They said she'd be back in two weeks and I didn't think you'd want me to wait around that long. But it doesn't really matter. I mean, I could see her fancy rooms, and I know she's well taken care of. Anybody would be with all that chocolate torte."

Esmerine struggled to breathe. "You can't really know if she's well taken care of if you never saw her! Two weeks?" Two weeks with a strange husband? Where was Dosia now? What was she enduring?

"Who was there?" Alan asked.

"Her husband's sisters. Proper human ladies with fancy

gowns and all that. They said I could stay longer, but I had to get back. Besides, I'm not sure I really like rich people's houses."

"What was wrong with it?" Esmerine asked.

"Well, I couldn't sleep at night. I had this bed that was huge and the whole place feels sort of haunted. Plus, it's cold up there, even in summer."

The picture in Esmerine's mind filled with images of cold, clammy rooms and ghosts, and Dosia lying awake and terrified in the darkness—beside some horrible human man who had kidnapped her—dreaming of home and bound by her belt.

Esmerine burst into tears. Ahead of her, the sky lit with a spear of sparkling light, followed by a group of colored blooms, but the beauty of the fireworks was lost on her.

"I'm sorry," Swift said.

She shook her head.

"I'll take care of her, Swift," Alan said. "You go and rest; it's a long flight."

Esmerine didn't even care who saw her cry. She'd been gone so long, and tomorrow she'd have to leave this place anyway, and none of it would matter. She'd known Dosia would be bad off—why couldn't she pull herself together?—but it was worse hearing it than just imagining it. Oh, waters, why why why? So many tears trailed from her eyes that she tasted the salt on her lips.

"Esmerine, shh," Alan said.

"I *won't* shh! I don't care, I don't care. That human bastard took my sister!"

"Let's just get you in the house. Put your arms around my neck." He took her hands and pulled them around his shoulders, and she tightened her grip, sobbing into the collar of his vest while he flew them to the ground.

She slid off his back and just stood there, still sobbing, feet stinging and aching with pain. She had cried for Dosia many times, but this felt like the first time, and there were other things mixed in too—the books, and Alan, and his wing around her shoulder on the roof, and how much she missed the sea and her family—

He slipped one wing under her arm and the other under her knees and scooped her up with surprising strength. His wings had always looked too fragile to carry her, but she realized now it was somewhat of an illusion. He marched her up the stairs and put her in bed, and sent Ginnia in to help her out of her clothes before he left.

"You rest now," Ginnia said when she had attended to her duty, leaving Esmerine alone on the bed in her sweat-drenched chemise. Her tears were running out, and she was quiet. Would Alan come back to see how she was? She wanted him to, but she wouldn't call out to him. If he had a heart, he would *know* she needed him.

She wanted her mother and father. Thinking of them set her whimpering again.

Alan did come back. He stood beside the bed a moment. "What do you want to do?" he asked.

"What can I do?" She wiped her nose on her sleeve. "I can't go after her. There is nothing to do."

"Well . . ." He sat on the edge of the bed. "If Dosia could get her belt back, she could be free."

"Yes, but we know that already, and it's useless information. She's north somewhere, I'm here, and where her belt is, nobody knows."

"What if you *could* go to her? Would you try?"

Esmerine pushed herself upright and leaned back against the pillows. "Why? How could I?"

"If we could fly together . . ."

"Surely you're not suggesting you could fly us both to the mountains?"

"It would be very far. I would need more magic than I possess."

Esmerine couldn't imagine flying to the northern mountains. It was almost too fantastical to consider even in a dream. "Does anyone have that kind of magic?"

"My father might," he said, his tone short. "Magic can be shared through an object. Just as your siren's belt is enchanted with magic you built up over time. He may have something . . . I've heard some Fandarsee are even hired to fly humans around in other cities. Most of the Fandarsee here would consider it beneath their dignity, but you are a different case. You're not just some traveling human."

She had had so many dreams where she could fly with Alan. In those dreams, she had flown all by herself, like she was swimming through the clouds instead of the sea. But this would be close. She could wrap her arms around him and see the things he used to tell her about. The red rooftops, the bell towers, the mountain peaks . . .

"But it's my father," he said. "He'll never agree."

"I couldn't anyway, I mean . . . my family expects me back, and—" But if she could bring Dosia home, what a triumph it would be. The joy it would bring the whole family was beyond imagining.

But it was an awfully generous suggestion for Alan to make.

"Besides, you can't just leave the shop," she said.

Alan scuffed his foot along the wooden floor. "My days here will have to come to an end sometime. My father wants me home. If I agree to that once this is over, I bet he would assist us."

It still seemed far too abrupt, and far too generous, for Alan to make helping her his last act before submitting to his father's desires. "No," she said, shaking her head. "Going home is one thing, but it's another to take me on some impossible trek to the mountains. I've seen no evidence that you even missed me!"

"It isn't . . . that I didn't miss you," he said carefully. "It's that I've been trying so hard to forget you."

To forget her?

"My visits to you were the most wonderful time in my life,

but they were an escape. I couldn't keep visiting you forever. Nothing could ever come of it. You know it as well as I do."

Her breath caught in her chest. "But—"

"We had a proper good-bye. It was best ended there. So when you turned up again—I didn't know what to think. I didn't want to remember those days. I didn't want another good-bye like that last one."

Esmerine had never known if he really missed her. At their last parting, she had wept and he had been stoic, saying again and again that it was for the best. Now she saw it differently. If he couldn't even tell his father he'd known her, he must have needed to act stoic, to go home and pretend nothing had happened.

"Are you saying you're willing to remember now?" she asked, still barely breathing.

"I'm not sure what I'm saying yet," he said. "You're a siren. I'm a Fandarsee. When you're here on land, you suffer. We can't reasonably be a part of one another's world, can we? But I can help you now. This once."

He really meant it. He would take her north to the mountains. It would mean flying even farther away from the sea. More days of legs and grime and chamber pots and hot food that upset her stomach . . .

But more days of Alan.

And a chance to see Dosia. Even if she failed to rescue her, at least she might establish correspondence. If Alan wouldn't bring her letters, maybe Swift would.

She met his eyes. He felt suddenly more present than he ever had, as if he was finally allowing himself to acknowledge that she had reentered his life. "All right. If you are truly willing to help me, then I will accept, with great thanks."

He let his gaze drop. "I should tell you something."

"Oh?"

"I'll be honest. It isn't entirely for selfless reasons that I want to help you. It's about my mother."

"Your mother?" She certainly had not expected that.

"My mother wasn't a Fandarsee. She was . . . like you. A siren."

Esmerine was immediately struck silent, and past her initial shock came a funny sort of relief. Alan's mother—a *mermaid*? Yet it explained so much—why he ate fish and seaweed, why he was immune to her siren song, maybe even why he had chosen to work at a bookstore run by a mermaid. It even explained why he tried so hard to be the model Fandarsee. But Alan's father marrying a mermaid? It seemed impossible. "How did that . . . happen?"

"I know," Alan said. "You saw my father. I can hardly believe it myself, and he doesn't like to talk about it. My mother died when I was four, so I never could ask her. I guess he fell in love with her during his own messenger days and stole her belt—or she gave it to him—he makes it sound mutual, but I can't be sure. She was very homesick in the Floating City . . . she couldn't fly and the other Fandarsee snubbed her."

"So . . . Dosia being taken by humans . . . I understand now why you want to help." Her voice was calm, quite unlike the turbulent emotions inside.

"I often think my mother would have rather been rescued."

"But then she had you. And yet, you can't even breathe underwater." Or was there more he hadn't told her? "Can you?"

"No. I can't. I'm Fandarsee through and through . . ."

But was he? Maybe he had the body of a Fandarsee, but he had come to visit her again and again, and even after their good-bye, he had quit being a messenger to work for another mermaid who must be just a little older than his mother, had she lived.

"The sea does tug at you a little, though, doesn't it?" she said.

"I guess it does. But I'm sure you know how useless it is to wish for impossible things." He stood up and cleared his throat a bit. "So, what do you think? Do you want to find Dosia?"

"Yes . . . but . . . I have to tell my family. Otherwise they'll be so worried."

"We can stop at the islands first, then go to the Floating City and ask my father for help. Hopefully all that will go well, and we'll proceed to the Diels."

"All right."

Alan left, and Esmerine lay in bed, knowing already that the night would be sleepless. For a moment, she imagined Alan as a merman—shedding his superior air and slipping under the water with her, strong arms and a tail replacing his wings and legs. The image was strangely abhorrent to her. Alan belonged in the sky, and he wouldn't be Alan without a book tucked in his vest.

If only—

She halted the thought. Tomorrow, she would fly with him. There was no need to think any further than that.

Chapter Fourteen

When Ginnia came to help her dress the next morning, she carried a bundle of new clothes in her arms—men's clothes.

"Mr. Dare suggested that you wear these for flying," she said.

Esmerine unfolded the pieces—a linen shirt, a storm-gray vest, dark-blue breeches, stockings, and knee-length spats like Alan himself wore. "I can put these on by myself, Ginnia," Esmerine said. "Thank you." She could hardly conceal her glee.

Esmerine would not have liked such clothes a week ago, when she was unused to wearing clothes at all—the tight spats and breeches made her more aware than ever of her individual legs—but compared to women's clothes, they were comfortable and easy to move in.

"Do they fit?" Alan asked when she came out.

"Maybe a little snug, but better than my other clothes."

"You're taller than my mother," he said. "I've been giving you her clothes, I hope you don't mind. My father brought me a trunk of them and told me to bring them to market for some pocket money, but I kept putting it off, and good thing I did."

"How do they look?" She did a half turn. "It feels so funny to wear boy clothes!"

"That's what Fandarsee women wear all the time," he said. "Dresses simply don't work, the way our clothes fit. So I don't see them as boy clothes at all. Oh, and you should braid your hair so it stays out of your face."

They ate a substantial breakfast and packed a bundle of extra clothes along with the winged statue, which Alan thought his father might accept as part of the bargain. Swift came around to say good-bye, as did Belawyn, who didn't seem as surprised as Esmerine expected. Esmerine still felt guilty for dragging Alan away from the shop, even if it was his idea.

"Don't worry yourself, my pearl. I managed this shop before Alan came along, and I'll manage it without him. Besides, thanks to your siren song this week, there's a little extra to go all around. Anyway, do you think I'll miss him and his meddling father?" She laughed, but when she told Alan and Esmerine to be careful, Esmerine knew she meant it.

"Don't do anything foolish, now," Belawyn said. "Don't do

anything I wouldn't do, and you might want to avoid most things I would do as well."

Swift looked the most upset. "It's too bad you can't stay longer. The customers were nicer because of your songs."

Esmerine smiled, but she knew she couldn't honestly tell Swift she'd be back, or that the shop would be just fine.

She gave them both a hug, while Alan offered a polite bow. "We ought to get going. Esmerine, are you ready?"

"I guess so."

He looked out at the nearly empty street. The sun had barely risen, and the hustle and bustle of daytime had not yet begun. "You've never been up so high before," he said. "You might feel scared."

"I might feel scared, you're right, but I've also dreamed about flying with you forever. I trust you."

Alan reached down inside the top of his spats and pulled out two leather loops. These were attached to the spats, and hung down about half the length of his calves.

"You can put your feet in these," he said. "That ought to give you a bit of stability. They are sewn into a lot of Fandarsee messenger spats in case we do need to fly with someone."

Indeed, she could step into the loops, like the stirrups riders put their feet in on horses. She didn't point out this connection because she had a feeling Alan wouldn't appreciate the comparison. This evened them out to a similar height, and she could wrap her arms around his neck without her feet dangling.

She took a firm grip on the collar of his vest again, more nervous than she cared to admit. Besides the flying itself, their bodies were pressed close, more intimate than she had realized. What Lalia Tembel said about the aroma of surface people was mostly true, but she still thought Alan had a nice smell, like books and hearth smoke and wool.

"Ready?" Alan asked.

She was trying not to breathe so hard. No need to be scared, she told herself. "Yes."

Alan spread his wings. The tips almost touched the buildings on either side of the lane. He started running, bringing her legs along with his, jostling her feet.

"Ouch, ouch!" she exclaimed.

"I'm sorry!" he said, and she could feel the wind stirring unnaturally, barely touching their hair but sweeping beneath his wings, catching the thin skin—too thin, it seemed to her just now. He leaped, and when his feet left the ground they did not return. His wings flapped; his legs straightened. His body was angled between vertical and horizontal now, and the ground was rapidly growing farther away. Red rooftops spread before them past Alan's shoulder.

"Oh my, oh my," she said. She almost wanted to close her eyes, but at the same time she didn't want to miss a thing.

They dropped. A sick wrongness rushed through her stomach that wouldn't stop, and her heart started beating so fast that she feared she would die. She screamed and shut her eyes. They were falling!

And suddenly the sensation was gone. When she looked, the ground was still getting farther and farther away.

"Don't choke me," he said.

She realized her arms had gone from his vest to his neck. She forced them back into their places, although even now the wind jostled his wings. "Oh my!" she said again. Panic rushed through her like the wind rushing over her.

"Don't worry," he said. "The air has currents just like the sea. Sometimes we'll drop a bit, but that's normal. Soon we'll be flying over the water, where the air is good, but until then it might be a little rough. There's more updraft later in the day when the sun has warmed everything up."

She felt better when he talked. He sounded calm. She realized this was as natural as walking to him. He flew somewhere every day and had never hurt himself, as far as she knew.

"Have you ever fallen?"

"Never," he said. "Relax. It's all right if your knees press into my wings a little bit. I'm leveling us out."

He dipped forward slightly, so they were now entirely horizontal and gravity held her safely against his back. The city spread below them as a panorama of rooftops and church towers, angling around the bay with the blue water beyond. Her heart was still pounding panic in her ears, but it was a beautiful sight.

"How long does it take to get to the islands?" she asked.

"Not long. Half an hour? Enjoy the view."

The sun was still low enough that the east sides of buildings were rosy, and the west sides shadowed blue. She was astonished at how lonely the water looked from the sky—it went on forever, and one couldn't tell at all how powerful the waves were. From here, they appeared as little white ripples. She felt so small, holding on to Alan, held up only by two delicate wings.

But it wasn't a bad sort of small. It was far more intimate than sitting on an island shore or even laughing on a rooftop. They might have been the only people in the world. They were free of all the trappings of earthly existence, just two bodies, shooting like the beams of the morning sun.

"Hold on tight now," he said. "We're turning."

His right wing lowered, while his left wing lifted. The wind swept them farther, higher, and then they dipped, more sharply than she expected, once again prompting a small shriek from her lips.

"It's all right," he said. "There's a good wind here, we just need to ride it. We're leveling out again." He turned his neck briefly to look at her out of the corner of his eye. "How are you doing? Are you scared?"

"It is a little scary!" She laughed breathlessly. "But it helps when you tell me what to expect. You sound like you know what you're doing."

"I definitely know what I'm doing. Although I've never carried a person like this. But we can make it to the Floating City just fine. Anyway, you're probably not that comfortable hanging on either."

"It's more strange than uncomfortable. Certainly better than walking around. And much faster than swimming. I can't believe how quickly you can get from Sormesen to the islands!"

"Just wait until we aim for the Diels. We'll be halfway across the country in no time."

Chapter Fifteen

As the islands where they once played came into view, the sirens' rocks grew visible farther out, where the bay opened to the sea.

Alan's head angled slightly down, giving Esmerine the sensation that she could shoot forward past his shoulders and splash into the sea. Her grip on his vest tightened. They seemed to be traveling faster now, although Alan told her it was an illusion of flying nearer to the ground.

"We're flying slower, in fact. Keep your grip!"

His wings angled sharply, with their heads aiming for the rocky shore of the island, and he veered to avoid a seagull. She moaned, restraining an urge to scream so no passing mer would hear them. Everything was growing very large very suddenly. It looked like they would shoot right past the shore and crash into the scrubby bushes—no, the trees—no, the big gray rock that they used to use as a stage—

And then suddenly the wind pushed his wings up, his feet hit the surface, jarring her own, and with a few quick steps, they were on the ground and he was pulling his wings in.

Esmerine took a few deep breaths before releasing her grip and stepping down on shaking legs. Alan put a steadying wing around her shoulders.

She panted. "Oh. Oh my goodness."

"We made it!" he said. "We flew together."

"Don't tell me there was any doubt."

"No, I've just never done anything like that before. I knew I wouldn't kill us, because I could always land if I had to, but . . . I didn't have to."

She turned from him, looking out to the sea. The sirens' rocks were still visible, very distantly, and she wondered if any of the sirens had seen her. The roar of the sea was in her ears, and her heart seemed to change its beat to move with the waves lapping at the sand, slapping the spot between the rocks that always caught them. A shudder went up her legs, and suddenly the urge to change into her true form was unbearable. She started yanking at the buttons of her spats—so many buttons!

"I'll stand aside while you undress," Alan said. He headed for the big gray rock, leaving a trail of prints in the sand. His movements seemed quiet against the wind in her ears. She sat down hard, sliding the pack with the clothes and winged statue off her back, and kept at the buttons. In a moment, she had the spats off. Shoes, stockings, and breeches quickly followed. Her legs were quivering and itching all over; she could hardly keep still. As soon as she had the breeches off, the change came upon her. There was no time even to get to the water. It was hard to believe she had spent a week in legs, and her body couldn't bear a moment more.

She sighed, giddy with the satisfaction of being a mermaid again. A wave of temptation swept over her, to slip into the sea and stay there, as she was meant to be. The sea had its own siren song. She had never realized, but now it sang inside her and she was under its spell.

She glanced at Alan, sitting about twelve fin lengths behind her on the rock, facing off toward the sirens' rocks. He had taken off his spats, shoes, and stockings as well, and was barefoot with his fingers clasped across his knees. The wind had mussed his hair.

She quickly unbuttoned her vest, flung her shirt aside, and pulled her hair across her breasts. "Alan!"

He stood and hopped off the rock. "Are you going? Don't be too long. The sooner we go, the sooner we'll be back."

"I won't be long." She scooped up a handful of sand and rubbed it along her arms, scrubbing off all the human grime.

"Do you think anyone saw us fly in?" he asked.

Was he nervous of the merfolk? As a child, he had never seemed so, but of course things were different now. Yet, by blood, he had as much in common with them as with the Fandarsee. "I don't know, but I don't think anyone will bother you. I'll hurry."

As if he had heard her thoughts, he said suddenly, "Don't tell your family about my mother."

"Why?"

"I just don't—I don't know. I feel out of sorts here. I don't like to talk about it."

"All right," she said, not really understanding, but he had only just told her about his mother; she wouldn't press him to tell anyone else.

She dragged and flopped herself to the waves, seal fashion, but once in the water, she was instantly fluid and free. Cool liquid carressed her skin, and her body was so light. She had always imagined flying must feel like swimming through the air, but now she knew flying was quite different—it was faster, with the wind skimming one's face, more perilous and exciting. If only Alan could come underwater with her too.

She stayed near the warm surface, and when she was some distance away, she looked back to see him on the shore, scrubbing his own limbs with sand. That made her smile. He didn't see her. Then she dove, flinging her tail above the surface before heading for the depths. Home.

Voices came through the small windows of the main room. It was still morning; usually her father was gone by now to fish, but perhaps he was scavenging today instead. She unfastened the door net and went in. The voices abruptly stopped and every face turned.

Her mother rushed to her and threw her arms around her. "Esmerine! Esmerine!"

"Did you find Dosia?" Tormy cried.

"Well, her husband took her to the northern mountains, just as the trader reported. So I didn't see her. But I've heard reports of her."

"How is she?" Her father motioned for her to gather around the table and share their breakfast, but Esmerine held back. She felt more like a guest than someone who belonged at the breakfast table.

"She's—well—I still don't know. I have to go to her. I have to see if she's all right. I didn't come to stay." When her mission was complete, maybe then home would feel like home again. Even without a single book.

"But how on earth can you go to her?" her mother cried. "You said she was in the mountains! Already all your lovely beads and bangles are gone!"

"Alan—Alander brought me here . . ." Esmerine had rehearsed telling her family not to worry. But she wasn't prepared for the look of disapproval on their faces when she explained the plan. Now she struggled. "He can fly me there. On his back. He'll take me to the northern mountains to find Dosia." It sounded ridiculous.

"Where is he now?" her mother asked.

"Waiting. On the island."

"What, he's here? Can we see him?" Merry had been too

young to go to the surface when Esmerine and Alan used to play, and had never seen a Fandarsee up close.

"Fly with you on his *back*?" Her mother's voice veered closer to a shriek. "That hardly sounds safe, or proper, or *wise*."

"I'm afraid I agree," her father said. "I understand your urge to find Dosia—we're all worried about her—but you can't know what you'll find. Besides, you might cause her trouble, if her husband is angry you've come around. Would you have a place to stay there? And as your mother pointed out, how will you pay for it?"

"I earned money . . . with my . . . siren magic," Esmerine said, her voice getting smaller as she tried to explain about the bookshop.

"Esmerine, daughter," her father said. "You must understand, it's dangerous to try and save Dosia. We all miss her, but if we lost you too, it would be . . . ."

Esmerine always caved when her father called her "daughter"—it meant he was at his most earnest. But this time, she just couldn't, despite the nagging fear he might be right. "I have to do this," she said. "I'm sorry. I *have* to try. I'm an adult now. My mind's made up."

"You're also a siren," her mother said. "You still have a responsibility to your community. You took an oath."

"So did Dosia, and she's gone forever!" Esmerine snapped. "I don't care if everyone disapproves, I have to find her. And I will come back, and then I'll be a siren until the end of my days!" As the words flew out of her, she immediately felt a sense of panic that it had been a lie, just like the panic she felt when she took her oath. Memories of conversations swirled around her mind, of Alan asking if Dosia was just an excuse to come to the surface, and Belawyn telling her why she had refused the honor of becoming a siren . . .

"I need to do this," she said, speaking more calmly. It helped her feel a little less alone to recall the conversation with Belawyn.

Some further attempts were made to reason with her, but Esmerine's family was eventually forced to accept that she would not be reasoned with. Instead, they insisted they would all return to the island with her to meet Alan.

Chapter Sixteen

Dosia was the only other member of the family who really knew Alan. Tormy had occasionally swum to the island to fetch Esmerine and Dosia for supper, but she was still little when Alan stopped coming. Esmerine's parents had only seen Alan once or twice and mostly ignored him. They weren't so unkind as to forbid Esmerine from seeing him, but since other merfolk made disparaging comments about the friendship, it had been a source of embarrassment they didn't want to encourage.

She wished she had some way of warning Alan, at least. She dutifully led her family to the island, but her movements felt mechanical, and her chest was tight with anxiety.

As they neared, Merry suddenly shot up to the surface to

try to get a look at him. Tormy followed in her wake. Esmerine jerked an arm out to stop them, then stopped. What was the point? They would all meet him one way or another.

"Did he see us?" Tormy said, diving back down.

"I don't think so. But maybe."

"He looks awfully odd."

"Esmerine, did you really fly on his *back*?"

Put like that, it sounded terribly naughty.

"It's too bad we have to meet him on land," her mother said. "How will we look to him, as he *looms* over us?"

"Maybe we should change into legs," her father said, although he was barely capable of walking and Esmerine couldn't recall her mother ever forming legs. It was something mermaids usually "grew out of."

"No, no," Esmerine said. "Alan is used to people wearing clothes." If they all came limping out naked, she'd never get over the embarrassment. "I'll—tell him not to loom."

No one wanted to come out of the water anyway. They poked their heads up as a group, close enough that Alan had to notice them. He started to get up, but Esmerine cried, "No, it's all right, stay seated! My family just wanted to meet you before we leave."

She had never seen Alan look so nervous. Between his bare feet and rumpled hair and wide eyes, he suddenly seemed quite young. "Hello . . . ," he said.

"What do we say to him?" her mother hissed at her father.

"Well. So you are Alander," her father said, lifting his voice over the wind, looking as authoritative as a merman could look with only his head poked out of the water. "Esmerine told us of your offer to help find our daughter Dosia. We appreciate that. But we are, naturally, concerned for her safety. And—"

Her mother cut in when he hesitated. "I can't help but wonder why you would want to assist her in this way. We wouldn't deny Esmerine a playmate as a child, but now—you're nearly a grown man." She glanced at Tormy and Merry, clearly regretting her decision to allow them to come along. Esmerine could hear them whispering about flying.

Poor Alan! Esmerine had often wondered if anything would ruffle him, and now she knew. He seemed at a loss for words.

She suddenly realized she was in the wrong place. She should be beside him, not her family. This was her decision, more so than his. She left the water and pulled herself next to him on the sand.

"I understand," he told her parents. "Esmerine expressed the same concerns. So I'll be honest with you as I was with her. It's true, Esmerine and I were childhood friends. But I want to help your other daughter to ease my own soul because . . . my mother was a siren, and my father took her belt, and she died . . . when I was four."

This silenced even Tormy and Merry.

"How could that be?" her mother said. "I've never heard of such a thing!"

"It's true, though," Esmerine said, cringing at her mother's lack of tact.

Her mother's face softened then. She looked as if she wanted to go to Alan and give him an embrace, but she couldn't easily leave the water.

"Did you know about his mother all along?" she asked Esmerine.

"I've only just found out," she replied.

"I saw no point in telling Esmerine . . . back then," Alan said, frowning at the sand.

"Can you breathe underwater?" Tormy asked. "Could you see our house?"

"No. I'm afraid not."

Esmerine's mother looked at him with pity in her eyes, just like the pity Esmerine had noticed in Alan's eyes when he had first seen her limp. She knew he must hate to see it just as she had. How funny, she thought, that they could each be the subject of pity.

"I see," her mother said. "I see now why you always came here. You should have told us."

"What would it matter if I had?" Alan said.

"Well—we might've—" Her mother looked a little helplessly at her father.

"We might've shut the neighbors up just a bit," he said.

After that, her family seemed to accept—although still grudgingly—that Alan's intention to help find Dosia was serious. Esmerine put her arms around all her family, a lump building in her throat that she refused to release, even when her mother and

Merry cried, even after she had put her human clothes back on and wrapped her arms around Alan's neck once more and watched her family turn small and distant when they took off. She closed her eyes and swallowed hard. It was not the easiest thing to talk about emotions while buffeted by the wind, braced for the next drop or wobble. Thankfully, Alan didn't talk either.

Perhaps a quarter of an hour later, the stone lighthouse on the point came into view, and the Floating City grew visible on the rocky cliffs of the island beyond, with the tiny forms of Fandarsee flying around it. When Esmerine looked down, she thought she could see the house where Dosia had been kidnapped, with the separate tiers of roof and the green garden enclosed in a square of walls.

She had seen the Floating City as a speck in the distance, but only knew the details from books. As they drew near, white shining towers rose up among individual houses and buildings; their delicate architecture seemed reminiscent of the Fandarsee themselves, their bodies more slender and graceful than that of humans.

"My house is up ahead," Alan said with a nod of his head.

He couldn't point out a specific one while flying. Hundreds of houses were built along the steep, wide paths, with the finest buildings rising highest. Most of the city seemed concentrated on one hill, but Fandarsee farmland was terraced in the cluster of hills around it. Windmills spun along the tops of cliffs. As they came into the city, winged traffic flew around them, keeping a safe distance, but seeing other bodies in flight made Esmerine dizzy.

As they swept over a broad square, she could see the colorful canopies of market stalls and the dark hats of Fandarsee gentlemen—the vision quickly replaced by the flat roofs of buildings.

She tightened her grip. Landings were her least favorite part, when the world came on too fast.

And then Alan's feet hit the surface of a broad, flat roof. She let out her breath.

He laughed. "You know, I think you've been remarkably brave for someone who's never flown before and isn't in control herself."

"I'm glad you think so. It *is* scarier than I imagined." She didn't want to think then about flying all the way to the Diels, but it would have to be done.

Alan turned toward a covered staircase on the roof. "We'd better go down. I'd rather go to them than have my father come to us, and someone may have heard or seen us land."

They slipped down the stairs and into a corridor. A door opened ahead, and a girl, her hair put up into two little buns, peered out. "Alan? It's you! Are you back?"

"Not to stay, I'm afraid."

"Who's with you?" she asked, coming closer. She wore breeches and spats just like male Fandarsee, with the ruffles at her collar providing a girlish touch.

"Alan, is this your sister?" Esmerine asked. She had

forgotten until now, but he had mentioned a baby sister when he used to visit her at the islands.

"Yes. That's Karinda. She's ten. Karinda, this is Esmerine. She's . . . a friend."

"A *lady* friend!" Karinda exclaimed.

"Shh!" Alan hissed. "I'm trying not to make a fuss about it. I just need to talk to Father."

"I'll come with you." She spoke very neatly for a little girl, just like Alan had at her age, with the same clipped accent. "He said you'd come home to stay soon."

"Maybe . . ."

"I hope so. Sort of. I want you to come back, but then you wouldn't have exciting stories to tell me about Sormesen."

"Oh, before long you'll be old enough to go to Sormesen yourself," Alan said.

Karinda was staring at Esmerine with open fascination even as she talked to her brother. "Did you bring me any smoked fish?"

"Not this time, but next time, I promise." Alan stepped past her, obviously eager to get the meeting with his father over with. Esmerine wasn't so sure she was especially eager, though.

"Alan, I can't keep up with you!" Esmerine said. Her feet were starting to burn from walking too fast.

"Sorry." He slowed his steps. "She's a mermaid," he told Karinda.

"Really? What is it like under the sea? How did you get here?"

"Alan flew me."

"That's the best way," Karinda said. "So you have a mertail? I wish I could see it! Do you keep fish as pets? What do you eat for lunchtime?"

Esmerine had always thought Alan was unusually mature for his age when they were children, but Karinda bore the same air of curious intelligence. Esmerine wondered if it might be the way of Fandarsee children. "I don't have time to talk about it now, but later I'll tell you."

The hall ended in more stairs, and the stairs brought them to a sparsely furnished room, all light and space and angles. What little furniture there was had a clear function: a desk arranged for writing, tall chairs gathered around a table. Aside from the ornately patterned floor rug, of the sort ships sometimes carried in bulk for export, the room had no decoration, but Alan could have spread his wings and still not touched the sky-blue walls, and such airy size gave it a sense of wealth. The wide windows had no glass, just wooden shutters formed of thin slats that opened to let in the light.

"Father's in the library?" Alan asked Karinda, who nodded.

"Karinda!" a female voice called. "Who's with you? It's lunchtime."

"Alan's home!"

A woman hurried out with a look of surprise that grew when she noticed Esmerine. Esmerine remembered her as the woman who had accompanied Alan's father in the bookshop. She guessed she must be Alan's stepmother.

The reason for their visit was given again, only now it was

Esmerine and Dosia who needed to be explained, rather than Alan. At first Esmerine was shy, unsure if Alan's stepmother would be disdainful of mermaids, but the Fandarsee woman looked at her kindly as Alan talked and offered them lunch when he had finished.

"Let me talk to Father first," Alan said. "Alone. The rest of you can start eating, if you wish."

"Your father might be grumpy if you keep him from his meal," his stepmother cautioned.

"He forgets to eat half the time anyway," Alan said. "Besides, I don't care, this needs to be discussed." He ran his fingers through his hair. "I'll be in the library."

Alan's stepmother smiled at Esmerine. She bore a strong resemblance to Karinda, although her brown hair was loose, the front pieces caught in a clip at the back of her hair. She wore a scarf around her neck that was fastened by a silver pin, but was otherwise dressed plainly, like her daughter. "We might as well eat. They'll be a while."

They adjourned to the dining room, another large space with simple wooden furniture, and painted maps hanging on the walls. Compared to the food Esmerine had eaten at the book-shop, the spread was lavish—sausage, corn mush and greens, sugared berries, bread still warm from the oven. Esmerine took a seat and reached for the berries. She hadn't eaten breakfast, but had no appetite for heavy food. Alan had never questioned her table manners, but now she kept an eye on Karinda to be sure she didn't misstep.

"So you've known Alan since you were children? What a surprise!"

Esmerine nodded. She hadn't expected Alan's stepmother to be so friendly and wondered how much she should say.

"That really explains a lot about Alan as a child. He didn't have many friends. I worried about him; in fact, he probably tired of me asking him about it and urging him to spend more time with other children. Imagine being friends with a mermaid! I never suspected he was keeping such a secret."

"I never *realized* I was such a secret."

"I'm just glad he wasn't as antisocial as he appeared, especially when his father doesn't always realize the value of fun." Alan's stepmother made a wry face, and Esmerine felt welcomed—one didn't make such expressions at unwanted strangers.

Alan's stepmother and Karinda asked her a number of questions about what she and Alan used to do and what life under the sea was like. It helped keep Esmerine's mind off of the raised voices she'd begun to notice from the next room.

Esmerine had just agreed to try a little sausage when the doors to the other room flung open and Alan's father entered. Alan came behind him, looking quite chastised.

"So," Alan's father said, scrutinizing Esmerine, no doubt comparing her to Alan's mother, Esmerine thought. "*This* is the girl."

"Yes, Father," Alan said.

"I'd like to talk to you both." He nodded and turned. His

tone gave no hint of his opinion of her. She exchanged a nervous glance with Alan and followed his father into a dim interior hall and through wooden doors that groaned heavily, ominously even, on their hinges.

As Esmerine passed the threshold, her head tipped back to take in a room that made the library Alan had brought her to seem small. Two stories of shelves filled these walls; a map of constellations spread across the ceiling. An inviting chair, shaped like a small plush bed, was placed before the fireplace, where, in the warmth of summer, charred logs lay unlit and patient. No matter where her eyes traveled, books and fascinating objects dazzled them.

Alan's father was looking at her oddly. "Has she never seen a library before?"

He knew perfectly well that she had; he'd seen her in the bookshop her first day in Sormensen!

"I told you she loves books," Alan said.

"And you know how to read?" Alan's father asked her, almost accusingly.

"Yes, sir. Your son taught me, for which I have been grateful all my life." It wouldn't hurt to toss out a compliment—or would it?

Alan's father harrumphed. "I can't imagine you've found much use for it."

"Maybe she can't read under the sea," Alan said, "but I like to think the things she learned from the books I brought her have served her well. After all, it allowed her to come to the

{ 155 }

surface world without being completely ignorant of what to expect. We had read so many stories, so many travel narratives, looked at so many plates of animals and monuments and fashions . . ."

"Is that where my best illustrated books were always running off to?"

Esmerine was listening, but her eyes were drawn to just such an illustrated book laying open on a nearby desk, with beautiful painted pages of animals or monsters of some kind. She forced her attention back to the matter at hand.

"It's very curious," Alan's father said. "You would almost think *she* was the child of a mermaid and a Fandarsee. Your mother certainly had no interest in books. She liked to look at the pictures, but she never wanted to read them. She wondered how I could stare at all those lines of words for so many hours."

"Esmerine is . . . not like other girls," Alan admitted. She hoped he meant that as a compliment.

"I cannot endorse your plans," Alan's father said abruptly. "I'm sorry. You know what comes of involving yourself with the business of sirens, Alander."

"Father, I swear I'll come home if only you'll help me this one time. For Mother's sake, if not for mine."

"Your mother is quite dead; there is nothing you can do for her *sake*. I appreciate the sentiment, but do be reasonable. I tell you, no good ever came of Fandarsee chasing after a siren; if anyone can tell you that with authority, I can."

"Please, sir," Esmerine said. "I have to find my sister and

learn her fate, only there's no way I can do it alone. Alander knew my sister too. We both just want to help her."

"I know all about your kind," Alan's father said. "If your sister has given away her belt, her choice is made."

They weren't getting anywhere. Alan looked defeated, Alan's father, dismissive. He had already made up his mind about mermaids, she supposed.

"Sir, I'll give you this statue if I can have an audience with you alone," Esmerine said, pulling the statue from her sack.

"An audience with my father? Alone?" Alan looked alarmed. "Why do you need to speak to him alone?"

"I just do. Please."

"You won't change my mind," Alan's father said. "And a moment of my attention is hardly worth a Second Empire statue. Sell it at market, don't waste it on an old man."

"Please, sir. I'm not trying to change your mind"—a lie—"I just want to speak with you a moment."

Alan's father huffed, then took the statue off her hands. "Very well. If you wish . . . Alander, go eat your lunch."

Alan moved to the door, but his head still pointed in their direction until the last moment. Esmerine twisted her hands but kept her back straight, trying valiantly to stay calm.

Chapter Seventeen

Alan's father turned to her. He reminded her of an eel—cold eyes and a grimace—so different from her own dear father. And yet, she had to convince him somehow.

"Sir, I know how this must look, and considering what happened to Alan's mother, I understand why you might be concerned about Alan following your path." Her jaw trembled as she spoke, but she didn't allow herself to pause. "But Alan and I are both aware of the trouble—" No, no. Wrong direction. "That is, we both have our own reason for helping my sister, and we're not doing this because—"

"My son clearly cares for you," Alan's father interrupted, his tone sharp. "Do you think I'm so stupid as to not notice the way his tone changes when he speaks of you, the way he grows nervous? Do you think I don't remember the way a siren's song can bewitch a man, make him lose his senses?"

"But—don't you see? Alan can't lose his senses. Mermen aren't affected by siren song, and Alan isn't either. Anyway, siren song works better on some people than others. I should know, I used it to sell books this past week, and not everyone bought them. It only plays on the inclinations people already have. Just like every mermaid can't become a siren. Only the ones who are enthralled by the surface to begin with."

"Are you suggesting that I had some inclination to marry a mermaid? A girl who couldn't read or write, and who knew nothing of cooking or managing servants?"

"That *is* how it works," Esmerine said, unwilling to say anything less than the truth, even if it angered him. "But I'm not like that. I don't profess to like books because I'm trying to enchant someone. In my heart, I *love* books, I love writing. I love the lines of letters on a page. Alan and I became friends because we shared that love. If we have any inclination toward one another, that's the reason—not because of a siren song."

Alan's father's expression didn't change in the slightest as she spoke. It made it hard to gauge what direction to take her words. "My son taught you to read?" he asked again, as if he hadn't quite believed it until now.

"Yes. I asked him to. He used to come to the islands and he always had a book. I wanted to know what was in them."

"And yet, it takes more than a shared desire for knowledge

to sustain love," Alan's father said, and the word "love," the gentle, treasured word, became a rigid thing on his tongue.

"We're not in love," Esmerine said quickly. "We just want to find my sister. We may have different reasons, but doing so will ease both our hearts."

"It is the way of sirens to leave home, isn't it?" he said, his tone growing bitter once more. "Why else do you keep your magic in such a way, and cast about with your feminine wiles? I'm sorry for your sister, but I won't allow you to drag my son along on some mad quest because you want to defy the very nature of what you are."

"But it isn't what I am!" Esmerine shouted. "And it isn't Dosia either! We always wanted to go to the surface world of our own accord. It wasn't to charm men; I'm so *tired* of people saying that. We wanted to see this world. Is it wrong to feel such curiosity? And what about Alan? His mother was a mermaid, yet he never knew her and he can never really know her world. But he must be curious too."

Alan's father sighed deeply. A hint of sorrow crept into his dark brows. "When he was born . . . a part of me hoped he would be a mer. And I would set them free. It was clear by then that her homesickness would never go away. But he was more Fandarsee, and she wouldn't leave her child."

Esmerine glanced, ever so briefly, around the beautiful library, and imagined a mermaid holding her winged baby, trapped by her love for him. First she saw her like a ghost, but then she imagined it was her own hand stroking the baby's hair. The baby vanished from the vision and she imagined herself standing in the library, knowing she had time to read all the books there. She was picking up that illustrated book and sitting in that plush red chair, crossing her breeches-clad legs, resting her aching feet, venturing into the world between the pages . . . *She* would not be unhappy here like Alan's mother had been.

Esmerine shivered, realizing it was no longer a vision of another woman, it was a wish for herself, a dangerous wish to wear the shoes of a Fandarsee woman, with all those books . . .

"Young woman," Alan's father said. "When I took Alan's mother home, I was dizzy with love for her. I never thought then about spending day after day flying away from her, going where she couldn't follow. I never thought about having to teach our son to fly by myself. And I never thought I would watch her die, begging for her belt so she could die a mermaid, begging for water, begging for someone to sing to her."

"Did you?" she asked.

"I don't sing," he said. "But Alan did. He sang every song she had taught him, until she was gone." He looked into her eyes, and his own were the same warm shade as Alan's. "Tell my son I want to speak with him."

She slipped out of the room, limping badly, thoroughly shaken. Alan sat at the table with his stepmother and Karinda, but he wasn't even holding a utensil despite the bowl in front of him. He stood as soon as she appeared.

"He wants to see you," she said.

"What happened?" Alan asked. "What did you say? Did he agree to help?"

"I don't know," Esmerine said. "He's waiting."

Esmerine returned to her chair, where her food waited, now cold.

Alan's stepmother smiled. "It's not just anyone who would talk to my husband alone. Good for you."

"It wasn't easy," Esmerine admitted, but she relaxed a little at the idea that she had done a brave thing.

"Did you cry?" Karinda asked. "Father always gives in when I cry."

"I think that only works for you," Alan's stepmother said, tweaking her bun.

"No, no crying," Esmerine said. "Though I might have, if we'd gone on much longer."

"Did you tell him what you'd learn from the experience?" Karinda asked. "He likes that too."

"I may have gotten closer to that . . ."

Alan's stepmother seemed to understand the topic was best left alone now, and asked Karinda if she had done her school-work. Esmerine had still not touched her food by the time Alan returned from the library. She understood immediately by his expression—serious yet peaceful—that the talk had gone well.

"He's given me the magic," he said. "We can fly to the Diels. In fact, we should get going. I don't know how fast the magic will allow us to travel to get her."

"Truly?" Could their journey really begin? It already felt like days since they left Sormesen, not hours.

A servant girl—also clad in a practical shirt and breeches—filled Esmerine's pack with bread and cheese and a thin blanket. There was no room for a second, but with the winged statue gone, the pack weighed no more than before.

Esmerine had never set out on a journey that would last longer than a day. As she watched Alan kiss his stepmother and Karinda good-bye, an anxious fluttering spread from her stomach out to her fingertips.

They went to the roof, the surface now radiating afternoon warmth. The Floating City made her think of a storybook—with its tiers of roofs and towers, it had the order and the tidy quality of a line drawing. More people filled the air than when they arrived: men, women, and children, some with books or hats or other parcels clasped in their toes. In certain congested areas Esmerine wondered how they avoided collision.

"Once in a while there's an accident," Alan said, seeing her alarm at the sky traffic. "But usually they manage to recover in the air. I don't think it's nearly as hazardous as those carriages tearing through the streets of Sormesen."

This time their ascent was quick and smooth, allowing her the brief delusion that she was getting to be an old hand at flying.

"We're making a sharp turn north," Alan said. "Hold on."

They passed over the Floating City. A flock of birds scattered from a tree below them and resettled in another. It made her dizzy to watch them and think she was higher than a bird in a tree. She closed her eyes until the feeling passed, pressing her nose into the back of Alan's collar.

Ahead, roads cut through fields where the tiny forms of men and women went about their work. "I never realized how much open land there is beyond the cities."

"Yes, you don't realize from the roads, but most of the country is just fields and hills, forests and mountains . . ."

"Have you been everywhere in the country?"

"Yes," Alan said. "My messenger route was usually from Sormesen to Torna. Sometimes to the eastern coast. A few times to the Diels."

A rippled blanket of hills stretched out ahead of them. If Esmerine squinted, the green tops of trees reminded her of the soft moss that grew on rocks under the ocean.

The sun rose higher and Esmerine guessed they had been flying for an hour, maybe even two. Her arms yearned to move, but she didn't dare release her grasp on Alan's vest. She fidgeted, wishing she could bend her legs or move onto her back or side, or even just escape the warmth of Alan's back. Anyone who might worry that flying together was romantic had it very wrong, she thought wryly.

"Uncomfortable?" Alan asked as she shifted again. "We'll stop, but we should try to make it farther."

Esmerine pushed her discomfort from her mind as best she could, but she was relieved when Alan decided to land. He brought them down in a grassy field, where they walked a short distance to the shade of a tree and ate their bread and cheese. Esmerine's arms trembled from gripping Alan's collar. And despite her aching feet, it felt good to have them on the ground once again.

"Will you make it?" Alan asked, scratching his back against the rock on which he leaned. He looked exhausted too. She imagined it was no easier to carry a passenger than it was to be one.

"I will."

"There's an abbey just through the trees where I sometimes stop to get water," Alan said. "You can walk with me or I'll bring you a cup."

Esmerine chose to wait, stretched flat on the grass, so tired of hurting but unwilling to admit it.

After food and water, they departed. She hated the idea of flying again, but she certainly couldn't complain about it in the middle of the countryside and after all the trouble they'd gone to.

Now the farmland looked endless, a patchwork of green broken by an occasional grove and the small block shapes of farm buildings with tan stone roofs reflecting the sunlight. Esmerine tried to relax her arms a little more, but it seemed that as soon as she loosened her grip, an unexpected current would make them dip or wobble, and her fingers would clench his vest again.

Despite her discomfort, she was struck by the endless beauty of the country, and by Alan, who kept them moving high and fast on his glorious wings.

"We'll have to stop in Calpurni," Alan said. "It's a little market town between farms. Should be safe enough, but . . . I don't know what the lodgings will be like. It could be very primitive."

He landed outside the city walls.

"It's not polite to bypass the gates in a small town that isn't accustomed to Fandarsee," he explained. "They get winged people stopping by sometimes, but usually we fly from Sormesen to Torna in one go."

Men in dirty, threadbare clothes rolled wheelbarrows out the city gates, while women carried baskets of food or yarn.

A few men loitered outside an inn, talking in a broad dialect Esmerine didn't understand. One spit in the street and another followed suit. Their eyes followed her feet, and moved up to her face, and one nodded to the other. "Pretty mermaid!" one called. "I'll give you something if you sing for me."

"I'll give you money," the other one said. "Then I'll give you something else." He laughed, and the other man elbowed him, but he was grinning too.

Alan put his wing around her, blocking her view of them.

"Hey, beautiful, I can't fly, but I've got big strong hands," one of them yelled as Alan hustled her in the door of the inn.

Esmerine imagined her whole face was the color of Alan's ears.

"If anyone asks, we are married," he whispered. "I'm not letting you out of my sight here."

She nodded, feeling very far from home, wishing she had no siren's belt. If men like them were to steal it in the night . . .

Inside, two younger men negotiated the price of lodgings with an old woman. She had the same accent Esmerine could scarcely understand, while the younger men were foreigners from Lorrine by the looks of their hats and sturdy clothes. A few Lorrinese tourists came to the bookshop every day. An old dog lay in front of a blazing hearth fire that contributed to the stuffy air of the room, despite open windows. Cheap religious art, yellowing and curling at the edges, adorned walls.

"You want a room, hmm? Haah? What sort of room would you like?" She jabbed a bony finger in Esmerine's direction. "She with you? She doesn't have the wings."

The Lorrinese man standing by the fire muttered to each other.

"She's, um, my wife," Alan said. "We want one room."

"Your poor wife," the old woman said. "She doesn't have the wings. I hope you take good care of her." She patted Esmerine's cheek, then waved them toward a staircase, as she discussed payment with Alan. Esmerine felt torn between laughter and irritation, but at least the old woman seemed to mean well.

The woman opened the door to a room that made Alan's house seem quite the palace. The exchange of payment was brisk, and Alan looked as grim as a man purchasing his own coffin. Finally, the old woman shut the door on them, leaning Esmerine and Alan to look at each other.

"Is this the only inn in Calpurni?" Esmerine asked.

"It wouldn't matter," Alan said. "They're all the same. You

can understand why I didn't last long in the messenger business with these conditions."

The room stank in some undefined way—not quite sweat, not quite mold, but close to both. The bed looked lumpy, with one thin blanket Esmerine already knew she wouldn't use. The open windows had no curtains, so any passing soul could poke his nose in, but the room would clearly be unbearably stuffy if they shut them. Through the thin wall, a man coughed incessantly, sounding quite as if he were in his death throes.

"I'm sorry I couldn't make it to Torna," Esmerine said. She felt she was to blame for the whole thing.

"I can't fly as far either," Alan said. "It isn't anyone's fault. We're here to help Dosia, not go on holiday." He flopped on the bed with an exhausted groan, one wing drooping on the floor. Esmerine unpacked the blanket, taking her time to avoid the inevitable question of where they would sleep.

"I can sleep on the floor," Alan answered before she could ask. "Just give me a minute."

"It's okay. I'm not tired yet. Not sleep-tired, anyway." She sat on a rickety chair by the unlit hearth.

The old woman knocked on their door and brought in their dinner. Esmerine would not have been surprised to learn that it had boiled for a week straight.

"I've seen worse," Alan said, attempting to poke a disintegrating potato with his fork. "This isn't likely to kill us."

It didn't kill Esmerine, but it did force her to slip through dark halls to the privy, not long after their first attempt to sleep.

The privy was dim and stinking, lit only by a high window, and she was trying to hurry through her business when she heard the Lorrinese tourists walk by. She didn't understand much of their language, but she knew the words "mermaid" and "Fandarsee," the former said with guttural lust, the latter with scorn. They sounded drunk and she froze with fear.

They talked in the hall for some time. She buttoned her breeches and stood, but was afraid to leave. It would be easy for one of them to grab her and the other to snatch her siren's belt. If she was gone long, Alan might notice and come after her, but would he be able to defend her against them?

One of them tried to open the privy door, which was locked with a hook, then pounded. "Who's in there? Go use your own pot if you're going to be all night." She heard laughter.

She couldn't very well stay in the privy all night. She swallowed and unlatched the door, prepared to bolt back to the room.

The man put a hand to her chest, keeping her back. "Look what we have here. We were just speaking of you. No hurry. We are friends."

"*Excuse* me. I need to get back to sleep." Esmerine spoke more boldly than she felt, shoving past the hand. The man made a grab for the waist of her breeches; fingers skimmed her back, but she ran, hot pain searing up from her feet. Her legs were on fire by the time she reached the bedroom, slamming the door behind her and securing the bolt.

Alan was on his feet. "Esmerine? What happened? I was about to go after you."

"Those men—in the hall—I ran . . . It hurts." She closed her eyes, inwardly begging the pain to stop. "They're still there." The men's conversation in their own language had resumed, not far from the door. The coughing man pounded the wall. They dropped to whispers.

Alan whisked the blanket from the floor and started folding it. "It's not safe here. We should stay out of the inns when there aren't other Fandarsee around. Especially here, with the window open like that. Anyone could get in!"

Esmerine nodded and helped him shove their things back in the pack. They were able to climb right out the window and take off with the Lorrinese men none the wiser.

"We'll just have to camp somewhere out of the way," Alan said. "I'm sorry." He looked out to the dark landscape ahead. "A forest might be a little too lonely. Maybe a vineyard."

He landed them between neat rows of vines laden with clusters of grapes that were pale and immature. A half moon cast just enough light to see the dark sea of vines around them, a distant white house, and shadowed hills beyond. The air seemed cooler here—not cool enough to warrant a shiver, but just enough that Esmerine thought it might trouble her sleeping.

"It's eerie, isn't it," Alan whispered.

She nodded mutely. Insects sang invisibly around them, but overall the effect was of a haunted place where the sun would never rise. She spread the blanket. "Now I wish we'd been able to carry two."

They both lay down on their backs on the blanket. Above them, the sky glittered with stars. Esmerine had rarely seen the stars because merfolk went to sleep when the sun set. Sometimes the sirens stayed up to guard the bay, but of course Esmerine hadn't been one long enough to be out late. She remembered one visit from Alan when he had told her about an uncle of his who was an astronomer. He had let Alan look in his telescope and see the moon. Alan told her about the moon, planets, and stars, and for hours they had speculated about whether there were other worlds with people on them, and whether gods—or God—Alan's people had a vague singular, while the merfolk talked in plural—were in the sky, or on the earth somewhere, or everywhere. It was one of the more intimate conversations they had ever had.

She looked at him now.

"Try to sleep," he said softly, although he didn't seem to be trying either.

She made a sound of doubt. "I'm still shaken up."

"It's my fault." He turned his head her way. "I should have thought this through better. The common human doesn't know a thing about mermaids except that they can be captured, and they think they have the *right* to capture them because mermaids sink ships. As for my people—well, we're better at fleeing than fighting, I'm afraid."

"Why do humans assume all mermaids want to do is sing and seduce them?" she asked, thinking back to Alan's father.

"It's all they know," Alan said. "They can't breathe under-water and find out for themselves, after all. They just know of sirens, sitting on the rocks and singing men to their doom."

"But we're not like that. Even your father thinks mermaids are stupid or only want to enchant men. He couldn't believe you'd taught me to read." Her eyes followed a shooting star. It was so easy to be honest in such a lonely, dreamlike place, under faint moonlight.

Alan was watching the stars too. He shifted one leg so his foot was on the ground and his knee was bent. "Maybe you could write a book," he said.

"A book?"

"About what merfolk are really like. Just like all those travel narratives where people talk about what the customs are in other human countries. You could write about what mermaids do, and eat, and wear, and what purpose songs and theatricals have in your society . . . talk about your myths and religion . . . There are a hundred things you could write about."

A *book*. She tried to imagine writing it—scratching out all those words on paper, watching the stack of pages grow, let-ting Alan read what she had written so he could learn about his mother's world. Then she imagined her words between two solid covers with gilt letters—not a big book, just a small one that Alan could tuck inside his vest. Maybe it would even have a few illustrated plates.

"I'd help you," he said, as if he had the same thoughts. "I know you've not written much before, but it would be such a unique subject that I feel sure I could find someone to publish it."

She caught her breath, momentarily overwhelmed by how wonderful the plan sounded. Except . . . "When could I write it, Alan? After we help Dosia, we both promised to go back home."

"You could write it while . . . Well, no. I guess it would take a long time."

"It would," she whispered. She might stay an extra week or even two, but more than that would be indulgent, and she couldn't write a book about her home in a week or two. She didn't know anything about writing, yet if she were to do this, she would want it to be as worthy as any of the books she had read. It would take time to consider what she wanted to convey. Disappointment crushed her chest.

She hated many things about the surface world, and yet there were moments that shone almost bright enough to make her forget her homesickness. It struck her that this vineyard under the stars would be a memory she'd hold on to for the rest of her life. She would think of it always—the time Alan had encouraged her to write a book.

But she had to say no. Someday soon she would look at the Floating City only from afar.

She turned away from him as her eyes welled with tears.

"Esmerine?" he said.

She wiped her nose on her sleeve.

He touched her shoulder, and she let him pull her onto her

back again. Now he touched her opposite shoulder, his wing draped over her, his eyes searching hers. "Don't . . . *cry*," he said. "It was only an idea."

"It's not that. I'm just . . . so scared. I'm scared I'll never feel this way again. When we were on the roof—and now—I kept thinking this might be the last time I'll feel alive like this."

And the way he looked at her at that moment . . . no merman had ever looked at her like that. So much emotion weighted his gaze—was it the same yearning she felt?

She put a hand to his collar, and when she tried to pull him closer, he didn't resist. In fact, he softened, like she had snapped some rigid piece of him with her touch.

Their lips met, warm and soft—and urgent. It was her first kiss, but it didn't have the lack of assurance that first anythings usually have. Her other hand moved to the back of his head. His short hair tickled her palm. His wing moved from her shoulder to her back, his embrace so sheltering that suddenly the vineyard felt like the safest place in the world.

She was still almost crying, even as they kissed, because she couldn't escape the thought that it would all be lost to her soon enough.

His lips parted from hers, and he touched his forehead to hers, breathing hard. "We can't—"

"Don't talk! Don't say it. I *know*."

His wing around her tightened, pulling her against him, so their skin was warm together through their clothes, and for a moment he held her like that, like someone might come and rip her from him if he didn't keep her close.

Then he let her go. They lay back down, but he kept his wing over her. She moved close to him. Nothing was said—they both knew it couldn't go on forever, so there was no sense in talking. She let her tears flow freely, quietly, for some time, and finally drifted to sleep with his wing for a blanket.

Chapter Eighteen

In the morning, they stopped in the next town for food: plump raspberries and bread laced with nuts, half of which was packed for later. Neither of them brought up the night before, but Esmerine noticed that Alan now touched her shoulder if he wanted her attention.

They flew over hills, their peaks growing sharper than the soft curves of the hills around Sormesen and the Floating City. By lunchtime, they reached Torna. Alan swept them over magnificent white ruins that dwarfed the ones in Sormesen, for Torna had been the capital of an ancient empire that had once stretched beyond the Diels in the north to the larger islands in the south.

North of Torna, they flew for a long time without seeing a town, just hills covered in vineyards and large houses with tiny people moving about them.

"We'll make it easily to Fiora late this afternoon. I do know a good inn there, so we should be able to get some sleep."

Once upon a time, Esmerine might have complained about the inn. Their bed there was ridiculously high, and the food lacked seasoning, but they had curtains—she would never take that for granted again—and such good wine that even Esmerine, who usually had no taste for the stuff, poured a second glass. There were other Fandarsee staying in the inn, which relaxed them both.

That night, with the wine loosening their tongues, there were no kisses nor tears, but laughter at memories of their shared childhood—memories of various games like shells carefully collected for currency to play "shop," the ongoing story in which they had pretended they were "friendly" pirates—as if there were such a thing—or the fact that their biggest fight had started over the rules to a game that involved swatting plants with sticks.

It was fun to laugh with him, but when they settled down to sleep she was more miserable than ever, thinking of the parting that must come. Sheer exhaustion claimed her quickly, but her dreams were fretful.

They departed Fiora under clear morning skies, and in the distance, looming like a mirage, were the Diels, their white tips turning golden under the rising sun.

"Is that really snow?" Esmerine asked. She had only ever seen pictures of snowcapped mountains, and it didn't snow in Sormesen. Esmerine had thought of the hills around Sormesen as mountains themselves, but she realized now how dramatic, almost frightening in their stark beauty, real mountains could be.

"Yes," he said. "The Diels are so high and cold that I can't fly over them. Fandarsee have to go through the passes just like humans. There's snow on the peaks all year round."

Esmerine understood why Fandarsee liked to live in warmer places. Humans and fairies could bundle up and tuck themselves around a fire during cold months, but mermaids and Fandarsee had no choice but to interact with their environment. Already the air nipped at her face.

But below them the hills remained hospitable, with towns climbing their forested slopes and broad valleys of farmland stretching in between.

By the time they reached the city of Tarinora, the Diels had grown to their full majesty, an abrupt shelf of mountain rising beyond the tiny hubbub of the city. Another Fandarsee was flying in. Alan angled closer, giving his wings a few brisk flaps.

"I'll ask him if he's heard word about your sister."

The other Fandarsee lifted a foot, acknowledging them, and slowed his flight until Alan flanked him.

"Alan, isn't it?" the other Fandarsee called.

"That's right. Darius?"

"From upper Torna," Darius agreed. "You've got a passenger?"

"Yes. We've come all the way from Sormesen," Alan said. "I'm looking for a mermaid who would have recently married a gentleman from this area, a Lord Carlo. Heard anything?"

"I've just come back from three months in Lorrine," Darius said. "But they may know at the messenger house. That's where I'm headed."

"I'll let you land first," Alan said. They were flying over dense rooftops now, with tiles a darker red than those of Sormesen. Darius swept down for a landing while Alan circled. Esmerine watched Darius set down on a rooftop, and as he did, Alan started bringing them in. Esmerine happily slid off his back, shaking exhaustion from her arms.

Downstairs, a dozen or so Fandarsee gathered, talking, reading, or drinking from large decorated mugs. The majority were men, but one man and woman talked together, and Esmerine thought the slender person reading a pamphlet by the fire was also a woman despite her cropped hair. A few of the Fandarsee had very dark brown skin, almost black. Esmerine had never realized there were so many Fandarsee from so many different places. As a child, she had assumed they all lived in the Floating City, and only consciously corrected herself now. Many wore similar blue clothing, which Esmerine guessed to be the messenger's uniform, and a few had even pierced their skin along the arms of their wings to accommodate sleeves.

So many dark Fandarsee eyes stared at Esmerine. And how young Alan looked among them! He had always seemed old and worldly to her, but many of the other Fandarsee had an aged and distinguished look, handsome but tired.

"Sit and rest while I ask around," Alan said, directing her to a chair near the girl with cropped hair.

Esmerine tried desperately not to look out of place while he went to the bar and talked to the men there. She was the only person without wings.

She watched the girl with cropped hair get up, stretch her legs, and give her wings a little shake, then tuck her pamphlet in her vest like Alan always did, before heading to the bar with lithe grace. A deep pang shot through Esmerine. How nice it must be to move with the ease of a Fandarsee woman, free of both human clothes and a mermaid's pain.

She stared at the fire for a time until Alan returned.

"I know where to go," he said. "Swift was here bragging about your sister's house. It's not far. Should we go there tonight or wait until morning?"

Her heart raced. "Maybe . . . morning. I want to see Dosia, but—"

"I understand."

The sooner they found Dosia, the sooner they would have to go home.

Chapter Nineteen

Although Esmerine had expected a grand house, the sheer size of the villa surprised her, while the Diels loomed in the background, dwarfing every human creation. Perhaps houses needed to look more monolithic here among the mountains. Nearly a hundred windows looked out on the lawn and its statuary. Alan landed them near the double doors so Esmerine would be spared the walk. Even as they landed, a servant hurried down the steps to greet them—or possibly to send them away.

Esmerine stepped down from Alan's back—clumsily, as she was now clad in a dress again—and resisted the temptation to stay behind him when the servant demanded their names.

"Alan Dare," Alan said, with a slight bow. "And this is Esmerine, sister of Dosia."

The servant smothered his surprise. He was a tall, grave-looking man in a white wig and black coat with gold braiding. Esmerine thought he looked adept at smothering his emotions in general. "Just a moment, sir. I will notify the household of your arrival."

Esmerine took a deep breath. "Goodness."

"Don't be intimidated," Alan said.

They waited. Birds landed on the neatly trimmed bushes of the garden around them, chirping to other birds that perched on the edge of the fountains. Esmerine understood why Swift had been so impressed. She imagined half her village might fit in the space the mansion occupied, and everything was impressively symmetrical. Each side of the path had a fountain, and if there was a bush formed of three round green puffs on one side, you could be sure it had its counterpart on the other side.

The door opened again, and Esmerine whirled around from gazing at the garden.

"Lady Carlo shall see you."

Lady Carlo! How impressive that sounded.

Alan offered a wing to escort her—or perhaps just so she had something to clench. They were shown into a grand hall, and Esmerine felt every muscle in her body trembling with the anticipation of finally seeing Dosia again.

Instead, two strange young women entered. The first had an imperious face with strong features, particularly her nostrils.

The second was freckled and sanguine, with an abundance of curls the golden-brown color of bread, and had the well-fed appearance characteristic of many humans. Mermaids were always very lean—fish and seaweed being a poor diet to put meat on one's bones. These women were both dressed in gauzy white dresses, and their hair was curled and styled in a fussy way so that some curls fell over their ears and some spilled from their buns along their elegant necks.

"Good morning," the imperious one said, her eyes roaming over them. "What a curious surprise."

"You are Dosia's sister?" the other one asked.

"Yes," Esmerine said. "Esmerine."

Esmerine only realized she ought to have introduced Alan after he introduced himself, with a slight bow. "Alan Dare."

"Christina Dantello," the imperious one said, "and this is my sister, Octavia. Lord Carlo is our brother."

The girls each dipped a knee. "What brings you to visit?" Christina asked. "You must have come a long way."

Esmerine thought Christina must surely already know, since she would have entertained Swift. "Well . . . to see Dosia of course."

"I'm afraid that our brother and your sister aren't here at the moment," Christina said. "They've gone to visit friends in the country."

"Gone?" Esmerine cried. "When will she be back?" She was beginning to wonder if Dosia had disappeared into the mountains forever.

"Soon," Octavia said. "Any day now."

Christina frowned slightly at Octavia. "Or it could be quite a bit longer. It's up to Lord Carlo. It's summertime and there are so many house parties and balls that he is hardly ever home."

"You're welcome to stay and wait," Octavia said, deepening Christina's frown. "Why don't we sit so we can talk in comfort?" She swept an arm backward, indicating they should adjourn to another room.

"If you don't mind," Alan said. Esmerine was beyond grateful for his generally unflappable nature, because she seemed to have lost her tongue completely. The party proceeded across the room, with Esmerine limping behind the group until Alan fell back with her. Everything had become surreal, the huge rooms and Dosia's absence and the sisters-in-law . . .

They entered a room richly furnished with couches upholstered in cream-colored silk with tiny green flowers, sumptuous red walls, and a massive piece of furniture that baffled Esmerine. It had a long, painted body and a similarly painted top that was propped open, and the legs were all gold and looked like birds of prey balanced on ornate perches. "Pianoforte," Alan explained quietly, catching her expression, but even he looked overwhelmed, she noted, when she saw his reflection in the tall looking glass over the fireplace.

Esmerine knew very little of human wealth, but she understood immediately that Dosia's husband had a tremendous amount of it. Alan's family had seemed well off, but nothing at all like this. The thought of stealing Dosia's belt back from this house made her shiver.

"Please do have a seat," Octavia said, urging them to settle on the couches.

"So, you can fly, Mr. Dare?" she continued, once they were seated and the maid had brought around coffee and platters of little iced cakes that would have easily fed ten people.

"Well, I would imagine so, Octavia, he is a Fandarsee," Christina answered. "You'll have to forgive my sister such silly questions."

"That little boy, Swift," Octavia said, "is he your brother?"

"Oh no, no," Alan said. "He's an orphan."

"An orphan!" Octavia clasped her heart and looked at Christina. "I told you we should have kept him around."

"How is my sister?" Esmerine said, growing unbearably impatient.

"She's fine," Christina said. "We're working on her manners."

"Manners?"

"Using silverware properly, how to address people, and things of that nature," answered Christina.

"She's gotten a lot better," Octavia said. "And her dancing is really coming along."

Christina made a small noncommittal sound.

A silence followed. Esmerine had no idea what to say. How could she ask anything important of these girls, like whether Dosia was happy and whether she loved Lord Carlo and he loved her? Even if they answered, it might not be honest.

Somehow the conversation plodded along, with the sisters prattling on about how Dosia was learning to dance and paint and how their brother got Dosia dogs, which Octavia pouted about a bit: "He knows I've always wanted dogs and he thought they'd make a mess." As much as the sisters talked, Esmerine never learned anything of worth, nothing about how Dosia really felt, if she'd come willingly, or if Lord Carlo had taken her away, as they had assumed.

When Octavia asked if Esmerine cared to stay, she hesitated, torn between wanting desperately to see Dosia, and wanting just as desperately to be alone with Alan again and away from the vast, opulent rooms and Christina's air of condescension.

"Esmerine . . . we've come this far," Alan said. "We ought to stay until Dosia returns."

Esmerine was panicked at the thought of staying in the grand house, but he was right. She couldn't give up now.

Chapter Twenty

Esmerine didn't have proper clothes for dinner, according to Christina, but Octavia said she could wear something of Dosia's. Esmerine limped after her, up a staircase that crisscrossed in the middle, with statues that looked like baskets of flowers for ornamentation.

Dosia's room was hung with tapestries and trimmed with yet more gold. A painting over the fireplace depicted a convoluted battle scene with rearing horses and men in armor, and more paintings adorned the ceiling. The bed had a canopy taller than Esmerine's head, with embroidered linens and curtains. The floor space seemed too large for the room, dwarfing even such a large bed, and a few chairs rested against the walls, lending an air of formality more so than comfort. There was no sense of Dosia there. Once again, Esmerine had the eerie feeling that Dosia had disappeared, that maybe she'd never even been here at all, and certainly she would not come back.

"How I envy your figure!" Octavia said, producing a dress. "You and your sister are both so elegant, like statues!"

"Except when I walk . . ."

"It must have been such a hardship for you to come. I remember when I first saw Dosia. We played music and showed her a dance, and she wanted to learn too, even though she was clearly in pain."

This felt like the first real thing Esmerine had heard about Dosia yet. "So . . . you saw her? When she first came on land?"

"Oh yes. We were all very interested to know what a mermaid was really like! Even Christina, although she pretended she wasn't."

"And my sister is married to your brother." Esmerine was trying to think of a polite way to ask if Octavia's brother had kidnapped Dosia, but it wasn't the easiest question.

"They seem happy, if that's what you're worried about." Octavia had rung the bell to summon a maid, and now the maid appeared and hovered around expectantly, so Esmerine let the conversation end. She hardly felt comfortable discussing her sister with Octavia, much less with a maid present. Could Dosia really be happy? Octavia and Christina both seemed to gloss over Dosia's feelings.

The maid helped Esmerine into a different sort of

undergarment. The stays were longer than she had worn in Sormesen, covering her hips, and made without boning, but they still kept her breasts pushed upward. A metal busk ran down the front, sewn into the stays, and kept her standing straight.

The dress was thin enough that she suspected her legs would show through the fabric in sunlight. It had an overskirt that split from the high waist, with embroidered sprays of blue flowers and a border edge of lace with a thin red trim. The skirt dragged on the ground behind her, most impractically. Esmerine thought of how Alan's wing would feel against her back through the gauzy white fabric, and her cheeks warmed.

The maid replaced her heeled shoes with leather slippers, and Octavia handed her a fan and a scented handkerchief. "You can borrow Dosia's," she said, as if Esmerine would need a fan and a handkerchief for something.

"You look lovely," Alan whispered in her ear as they entered the dining room. But even a compliment wasn't enough to make up for the excruciating dinner. The room was gloomy, with an intimidating number of servants and dishes and utensils, and the food repulsed Esmerine. Dark-colored meat came in huge hunks on the bone. Fish never had such large bones; these could have been the bones from her own arms, and the flesh was hearty and fatty and smelled unfamiliar. She had eaten small quantities of meat at Alan's or in the inns, but never such hunks of it.

She was picking at her rice, trying to make it look as if she had eaten more than she actually had, when they heard voices and laughter in the hall.

Octavia beamed. "I told you they'd come back tonight!"

Esmerine stood, ready to rush at Dosia and embrace her, but it quickly became apparent that there were many more voices than just Dosia's or Lord Carlo's, and she sat down again as a boisterous group entered the room, with Dosia among them, two little dogs running around her feet. Dosia was glancing back at one of the men and saying, "I'd like to see you try *that*, sir!"

Everyone was still laughing as Dosia's smile drained into shock at the sight of Esmerine.

"Esmerine! And—and *Alander*?"

"Yes," Esmerine said, just short of speechless.

"I don't believe it! Why are you here? Is everything all right?"

"I might ask you the same!" Esmerine cried. "Everyone back home is worried sick."

"Oh my goodness," Dosia said. "Let me get a good look at you." She hurried around the table, light on her slippered feet, as if she had been born to legs. Esmerine stood again to embrace her. Dosia smelled like perfume and cool mountain air, and she was dressed so finely, in a beribboned bonnet and a little green velvet jacket and gloves of fine leather.

"Everyone, this is my sister Esmerine!" she announced to the crowd in general. "Esmerine, you can finally meet Fiodor, my husband." She tried to tug Esmerine forward, but Esmerine couldn't move so quickly. "My feet," she said softly.

"Oh! I'm so sorry! I forgot," Dosia said.

"You *forgot*?" Esmerine's arm flinched from Dosia's grasp. Then she thought she was acting poorly, and she forced a smile. "I'm sorry, it's all right."

"Well, that is Fiodor. Or 'Lord Carlo,' if we are being proper."

"In-laws," Fiodor said. "You could have warned me! I thought I was safe." He winked at Esmerine. His appearance surprised her; he didn't seem Dosia's type, or perhaps it was that he seemed so hairy compared to mermen, with a head of dark curls and a stubbled jaw. Alan had a sharp precision to his accent and features, like the blade of a knife, but Fiodor reminded her of a rock on the shore—craggy and strong.

"And I suppose you're acquainted with Christina and Octavia, since you seem to be having dinner with them! But let me introduce you to the rest of our friends, here visiting from Ibronia—"

All their names immediately escaped her. There were three single men, a married couple—newly married, judging by their constant giggling and touching—and the younger sister of the wife. Both men and women were loud and cheerful, settling into chairs the servants produced, and asking an exhausting number of questions of Esmerine and Alan and everyone else. Esmerine didn't want to answer the questions of strangers. She wanted to get Dosia alone and ask questions of her. But it seemed she must continue to wait. More platters of food came out, and the wine glasses never ran dry.

"Are you two married?" the wife asked Alan and Esmerine at one point, wiggling her finger from one to the other.

"Oh no, no," Alan said. He was sitting beside her but seemed very far away. All the closeness of their journey had evaporated, and now they were just two people enduring a situation.

"Now, I've always wondered about mermaids," one of the men said, clearly halfway to drunk, raising his eyebrows suggestively. "They're girls, but also fish. Can't say I've ever wanted to seduce a fish. Why are mermaids supposed to be so much better than regular girls?"

"Because their legs are all the more attractive for being hard to get," Fiodor said, reaching over with a broad gesture and squeezing Dosia's thigh.

"Be good," she said. "My sister's here." She added, "We're better because you have to tame us."

"Now, *that* just isn't possible," Fiodor said. The guests laughed.

"Know that from experience, eh?" the drunk man said.

Dosia shot him a mischievous look, to a chorus of hoots.

Esmerine was staring wide eyed at her plate, wishing her chair would drop right through the floor. Dosia seemed like a stranger, as if Fiodor had been the one to enchant her and not the other way around.

Christina quietly stood up. "Excuse me. I'm going to bed before this all gets out of hand."

"Now why would you want to leave a gathering just as it's getting out of hand?" the younger woman cried. Esmerine thought her name was Ambra.

Christina gave her a look of disgust and left the room.

The guests shared stories of ghosts and seemed to delight in making Ambra screech with horror—in fact, the screeching seemed put on, an excuse to clutch the young man beside her.

The sun had gone down long before the dinner finally ended. The servants had trimmed the candlewicks several times as they burned down, lighting everyone's faces golden. Esmerine lost track of the courses—after the rice and meat there was candied fruit and blue-veined cheese, then little cups of sweet, thick cream and round almond-studded cakes, followed by hot chocolate, and finally dessert liqueur. Once again, the food was abundant as if the guests had all been expected. When each plate came around, Dosia explained what it was, but after a while Esmerine stopped caring—each dish simply had to be consumed and persevered through.

Everyone left the table energetically, except the drunk man, who lolled back a moment, his face red. "Get up, man," Fiodor said. "We'll play some cards."

Esmerine hung at the back of the crowd, clutching her stomach as she limped along. How could this be her sister? Her sister's life? How could Dosia be smiling and laughing?

Alan slipped back behind the laughing Ibronians to walk with her. "Are you all right?"

"The food was so rich."

"Tasty, though."

She nodded but didn't really agree.

"It isn't my crowd either," he whispered. "Then again, I dislike crowds as a rule. But if we're here to—"

"I don't know what we're here for," Esmerine said flatly. "Dosia's different."

"Is she? Even as children, I could see that she was more sociable. Louder, certainly. She was nearer my age than you were, you know, but I didn't come to see her."

Esmerine bit her lip. "Well, she wasn't like this. I don't know how she could just— I mean, it's like she doesn't even care that she left our family, and no one knew if she was all right."

"I'm sure she cares. She must be torn between trying to be one thing for you and another thing for her new family."

A lump rose in Esmerine's throat. "Don't call them that."

"You're different too," he said. "That must be part of it. You two were always close and now you've been without her for . . . how long?"

"Two and a half turns of the moon . . ." It was true. She had learned to live without Dosia in some ways. When she thought of Dosia with their friends back home, perhaps Dosia's behavior was not so different. She had always been flirtatious and willing to go along with anything. It was the humans that distracted Esmerine—they were not like merfolk. The house wasn't home. The food was all wrong.

"I just . . . miss home," she said softly, unsure what home even meant anymore.

The party had reached the room with the pianoforte. Candles in mirrored wall sconces and several candelabras provided the room with soft light that reflected off of the gold decorations and made their white dresses glow. Octavia settled at the bench to play, and Dosia waved Esmerine to sit beside her. Servants brought around wine and chocolates. Esmerine couldn't believe anyone had room for more food, but the party greeted the platters as if they hadn't seen sustenance in hours. Ambra and her gentleman occupied the couch, making lusty conversation with their eyes alone. Fiodor clapped with the music. The drunk man grabbed the wife—unattached while her husband slipped away to the privy—and whirled her around the room's open space. Alan stood against the wall and seemed to be making a futile effort not to stick out.

Esmerine let her eyesight blur and tried desperately to imagine she was under the water, and nothing had changed so very much. She tried to tell herself she belonged here, in this moment. It was real. Her sister was here, and she was here, and when she went home, Dosia would still be here, and that would be fine. It was normal to get married and leave home, even to a stupid human. Well, whomever Dosia married, it would have been stupid. Esmerine was too sensible for things like that, except with Alan, and even then she was sensible enough to know it could never really *happen* . . .

All the anger she felt when Dosia ran away was bubbling up now. She clenched her hands on her lap, stomach gurgling, hating everything.

"Esmerine? Are you getting sleepy already?" Dosia touched her arm. Esmerine hadn't even realized how far afield her thoughts had drifted. "We're going to play cards. I can teach you."

"Oh . . . no." Esmerine stretched her arms over her head. "Could we . . . speak alone?"

"Well, a hostess isn't supposed to leave her guests alone, but I suppose these are extenuating circumstances. I'm dying to know how you came to find Alander again! And how handsome he's grown up to be!"

Esmerine shot Dosia an eyeful of her anger. "I didn't come here to talk about Alan!"

Dosia's lips twisted in an apology. "All right. Well, let's go to my room and talk. I just need to tell Fiodor."

Esmerine sat for a moment, jaw clenched. She needed to say something to Alan too, but it was hard not to simply burst into tears. She briefly caught his eye, and he swept to her side as if he'd been waiting for a signal.

"Should we leave?" he whispered. "You look utterly miserable."

"No. I need to talk to Dosia first." Esmerine glanced behind her. Dosia was laughing at some joke of Fiodor's, which sent a new lance of anger through Esmerine's heart. She grabbed Alan's elbow. "Let's talk in the hall. I can't spend another moment in here."

They left the room together. Laughter went on behind the doors, but the dark quiet of the hall had a substance that seemed to hold back the sound.

"I'm sorry I dragged you here," Esmerine said.

"You didn't. I offered."

"You didn't have to—I don't know, it's just, you've hardly

said a word all evening, and I've been trying to go along with everything . . ." She gasped for a breath. "I miss moving freely, without pain. I miss being *me*."

"It's understandable," he said in a careful tone, obviously seeing how close she was to breaking down entirely. "But I think you'll feel better when you talk to Dosia alone and she can be honest with you. She seems happy here, at least."

She didn't want Dosia to be happy here. And she didn't want him to leave her alone with Dosia, but she couldn't say that. She rubbed her throat, which had tightened from keeping back crying, and managed a sigh.

"What do you want me to do?" he said.

"I don't know. I wish we'd never spent that night in the vineyard."

"Why?" he said, but he looked like he already knew. He took one step closer to her, and more than anything she wanted to fall into his embrace and repeat that kiss, but at the same time . . . oh waters! She felt like driftwood tossed about a stormy sea, and no one could make it all right. The safe and right thing to do was to go home now that she knew Dosia was okay, so why did it seem like such an awful prospect?

"I can't stand it now. As if I could go home and just sit on the rocks all day for the rest of my life and forget about you."

"Then—then don't go." In the dark hall, lit by a single candle, his expression was a solemn shadow, his voice soft and intimate, almost as if he whispered in her ear over the muffled chatter and joyous shrieks in the next room.

"But . . . how can I stay?"

"Because I can't follow you. It doesn't matter how much I might wish it, I *can't* follow you." His teeth were gritted.

"That's not true. You were the one who came to me all those years. You stopped coming, and you said you'd come back when you were done with the Academy, and you never came back."

"I told you why I didn't return. But it doesn't matter. I can knock on your door, and you can stand there and chat, but you can never invite me in. That's what it's like. Standing at your door like a hopeless idiot while everyone you know passes by to stare."

"But would you really follow me if you could? Would you give up your wings to follow me to the sea? Your family? Books and paper? Everything?" A few soft tears finally dropped from her eyes. "I wouldn't even want you to."

"No," he said. "I don't want you to sacrifice for me, either. I don't want you to come to my world where you don't fit in, or have winged children and stay for their sake, even if I were to die. I don't want your feet to hurt, and I'm absolutely sure I don't want to take your belt, and I know you would have to give it up to be free of the pain you feel on land. I don't want to love someone who had to sacrifice so much of herself to be with me."

What was there to say? There were many reasons to care for Alan, but from the first time she saw him she had been fascinated by his wings, and all that they meant—the ability to speed through a mysterious world, to spread knowledge. The birthright of a Fandarsee. And surely Alan was just as attracted to the world she represented—a world equally mysterious to him, and equally beautiful.

"Esmerine," he said. "There's no good in this talk. You came to see your sister, and you need to speak with her. And I should go spend the night at the messenger post, but I'll be back first thing in the morning, I promise."

Esmerine knew he was right. She remained silent, fighting to rein in her emotions.

"I promise," he repeated. He touched her shoulder, briefly, and she moved toward him with an almost instinctive yearning, but he was already turning away as Dosia slipped into the hall.

Chapter Twenty-One

Dosia squeezed Esmerine's arm. "Oh, Esme, don't be cross! I've missed you so much, and we've got so much to talk about. We'll cozy up in my room away from all this and drink some tea. You'll feel so much better."

"I don't want tea," Esmerine said. "I don't want to eat or drink one more thing."

"All right," Dosia said soothingly. "We'll just talk then."

They moved slowly up the stairs. The two little dogs came hurrying out from somewhere, panting noisily, edging their noses under Esmerine's skirt, huffing out small barks.

Dosia snapped her fingers. "Down! Go upstairs! Dominic! Frederico! Good lads." She smiled crookedly at Esmerine. "I'm so sorry. They were a wedding present from Fiodor and they're not really trained. But they're well-intentioned little things. They distracted me from my homesickness quite a bit."

Esmerine stared at the ground. Her stomach still felt ill from the rich food, and her feet were burning. It was easiest to think of these things.

Dosia sighed. "Oh, Esmerine, can't it be like old times for tonight? I so want to know how you got here. How did you find Alan? Was he happy to see you?"

"I'm not talking about Alan! Not until you tell me every-thing! We've all been worried sick about you. And being a siren has lost all its luster. We were going to do that *together*. Every-one told me I shouldn't come after you, so I tried to keep going along as if everything was normal. But one day the traders said your husband had taken you away to the mountains to keep you from the sea because you were so homesick. It broke my heart. And now I'm here and you're laughing and flirting and running around with dogs and it seems like you don't even care how much you've hurt us all! Why didn't you send word?"

"It's not as if I can just post a letter. I can't even write myself, and I'd have to figure out a way to be sure it got to you. And it was so hard to figure out what to say."

"Well, you could have . . . tried."

They reached Dosia's room. Dosia quietly asked the maid to light the candles and leave them alone.

"I'm sorry," Dosia said. "I guess I didn't think how it would affect you all. I suppose I flung myself into my new world a

little too hard. I don't want to seem like a weepy little merwife."
Dosia suddenly clamped Esmerine into another tight hug. "I'm
so sorry," she repeated. "I never thought I'd see you again. But
I'm so glad you came to see me. Did Mother and Father want
you to come? Do they even know you're here?"

"Yes," Esmerine said. "I'm here with their consent.
We couldn't rest without . . . knowing. I mean—you were
kidnapped. Your husband . . . is he . . . ?"

Dosia stepped into the bedroom. The candles cast eerie,
flickering light in the overlarge space, illuminating the tapestries, and Esmerine could see why Swift had been frightened.
"Esmerine, I . . . I let Fiodor come close." Her color had deep-
ened, and Esmerine understood with a sudden jolt that she had
been mistaken all along. Dosia hadn't been kidnapped. She
had gone willingly. She had left them all behind.

When Dosia was fourteen, she had her first beau, a skinny
boy to whom everything was a joke. Esmerine hated how Dosia
only wanted to talk of Baroden instead of playing games or
anything else.

One afternoon Esmerine had come across Dosia and
Baroden in a cave, tails twined, hands and mouths all over one
another. Esmerine had screamed, horrified by the sight, and
run to tell her mother, who had severely scolded Dosia for such
inappropriate behavior and confined her to the home cave until
the next turn of the moon. Dosia and Esmerine had the worst
fight of their lives, but Esmerine had always felt in the right.
She had never understood why Dosia wanted to get so close to

a boy, and in secret, at that. Why couldn't she just behave herself?

"You gave him your belt?" Esmerine whispered.

"I did . . ." Dosia met Esmerine's eyes. "That last night at home, when I told you about them . . . I thought you'd be more curious. I thought you'd come with me. I didn't intend to run away then, but I wanted to see him again, and I was afraid you'd try and stop me. And then—well, Fiodor told me he'd have to go home to the mountains, and I couldn't bear the thought, and everything just happened so fast."

"You willingly gave your freedom away to a man you'd only just met?"

"I chose this," Dosia said. "You don't understand these things. I don't think you ever have, and you always made me feel ashamed when I did, but I can't help being attracted to boys, and Fiodor's rich and lovely and I knew I'd never have another chance like this."

Esmerine couldn't believe Dosia would make her sound like the strange one. "But how can you ever know if he really loves you, if he's enchanted?"

"Does it really matter, if we're both happy?" Dosia said. "Anyway, what are you going to do about your situation?"

"*Me?*"

"Yes, about Alander. Don't pretend as if there's nothing going on. Even as a child you were mad about him, and he must have gone to a lot of trouble to bring you here. Don't you think it's amazing that you found him again?"

"Well, it was lucky, but that doesn't mean anything," Esmerine said sternly. Dosia was twisting everything, trying to get her to stay on the surface world so she wouldn't be alone, wouldn't be the only irresponsible one. "And even if there was something there, what about Mother and Father? Do you expect me to go back and tell them we're both going to leave them?"

"Maybe they'd feel better if they knew we were both happy here."

"Are you really *happy* here?"

Dosia perched on the bed between the dogs, stroking their heads in unison. "I think so."

"When we talked about coming to the surface world, it wasn't like this."

"No. That's true. But things don't have to work out like we expect to be good. I feel like you want me to say I'm happy all the time, and I'm not. I still cry sometimes, and I'm still getting to know Fiodor, and some things are strange. But I will tell you this . . . even though I never imagined it would turn out quite like this, I think I always meant to end up in the human world. I miss you desperately. I'm glad you came. I just wish you didn't have to go."

Esmerine sat on the bed and drew her legs up to her chest. "I feel like I've lived years since you left. I was going to be a siren, and everything was *fine*— No, everything wasn't fine. When I said my oath, I was terrified. It wasn't exactly what I wanted, but I never thought I could have what I really wanted." She lowered her head, letting her hair fall around her face.

"Now I'm terrified because . . . I've seen what I want. But I still can't have it. I can't give Alan my belt."

"Why not? If you want to spend your life with him . . ."

"He doesn't want it. I can't live my whole life in pain . . . but neither of us want the burden of enchantment between us."

"Then you'll have to decide," Dosia said. "I *know* it isn't easy. I can't tell you what to do either. It's obvious what I wish you would choose, but only if it's what you really want. I just wonder . . . could you really go back home, now that you've seen a glimpse of that other life? That was the question that sealed it for me. Even though I'm sometimes homesick here, whenever I ask myself that question, the answer is always the same."

Esmerine dropped her feet back onto the floor. Even then she could feel a hint of pain. There would always be pain for her here. She could never forget that mermaids belonged in the sea. But Alan couldn't follow her there.

Dosia threw back the bedclothes and slipped her feet between the sheets. "Maybe we should get some sleep. Things will seem clearer in the morning."

Esmerine obeyed, but she doubted she would sleep much. She had already fallen to sleep quite a few times pondering the same questions, but the answers remained elusive.

Chapter Twenty-Two

The next day the sky was a brilliant blue, with great complicated puffs of clouds, perfect for imagining shapes. Dosia declared that they simply *had* to spend the day out of doors, and quickly silenced the grumbling of last night's drunken man, who was now quite a regretful sight, clutching his cup of coffee and groaning periodically. He seemed to be hoping—without luck—for some female sympathy.

Alan arrived during breakfast and sat beside Esmerine, but he didn't speak beyond exchanging greetings, and she found herself suddenly shy around him, even when, as usual, they walked together at the back of the group on the way to the picnicking spot.

Dosia led the party farther than Esmerine expected, past the gardens and into the woods. The trees were tall and sheltering, and the path underfoot thick with leaves. The trees whispered in the wind, which made the laughter and loud voices of Dosia and Fiodor and their friends seem disrespectful. Esmerine looked up at the sun, dappling through the dark branches, casting spots and lines of gold on her arms.

"Esmerine . . . you've never been in a forest, have you?" Alan asked.

"No. It reminds me of being underwater, the way the sun comes through . . . It feels softer here."

"My favorite forest is north of Torna," Alan said. "Maybe on the way back, we can stop and eat. I see the most wildlife there—lynx, bear, foxes, deer . . . but the real prizes are the mushrooms."

"I've never had a mushroom."

"I have a secret spot for chanterelles. I don't think the other Fandarsee know. Ginnia makes them with butter and white wine." He sighed softly. "Too early in the season for them now."

"Esmerine!" Dosia made her way back to Esmerine's side, a basket draped over her arm, displaying a palm full of small strawberries. "We're berry picking. They look like this and they're everywhere. Then up ahead we have blackberries. Or if you need to sit down, the servants are setting up a canopy, and I can bring you some berries."

"I'll pick." Esmerine badly wanted to explore the forest. If she decided to go home, she only had a few days left to experience the surface world, and if she decided to stay and keep her belt, she would have to endure pain or she'd never see anything.

"Here, take my basket," said Dosia. "The servants have more."

Picking berries proved the ideal activity, because Esmerine and Alan could break off from the noisy group and make simple conversation about spotting fruitful bushes. Esmerine enjoyed filling her hand with berries, small and sweet and bright. Occasionally, they exchanged a tacit glance, as when one of the women exclaimed, in a voice loud enough that it had already scattered a pair of birds, "I can't believe we haven't seen any deer!"

Alan had more trouble with the blackberries, as his wings were too unwieldy to weave between brambles and snatch the more elusive prizes. She could reach most of them, although her stays prevented her from reaching over her head. They worked together until her arms were mapped with thin scratches. The brief pain of snagging a bramble was almost satisfying, because she had something for her troubles at the end of it.

Her aching feet could be dealt with, moment by moment, but after over an hour of wandering from bush to bush it grew exhausting, and the sun was climbing—proving hotter than expected, as the others kept exclaiming—bringing on sweat and thirst. The breeze that periodically rustled through the bushes couldn't overcome Esmerine's layers of clothes, especially her stays.

Esmerine lay down upon the blanket, beneath the white canopy erected in a broad patch of grass. The servants had set up a few folding tables around it and were bustling to and fro with food and pitchers of beverages. They offered her a cup of lemonade, tart but refreshing. A thick cluster of clouds slid over the sun, bringing blessed relief from the heat. Soon enough, the rest of the party joined her, exclaiming over the heat and the bounty of berries. Esmerine let their feet thump around her for a moment while her thoughts floated far away.

Dosia sat nearby. "You'll feel better once you have some lunch."

Esmerine was not at all sure of that, but she tried to perk up. She watched Alan attempt to settle himself on a corner of the blanket—without chairs, he had to carefully fan his wings behind him.

Despite the informal setting of the picnic, the servants still got up an impressive spread of fruit, bread, slices of cheese and meat, sausages, corn cakes, buttery pastries, and chilled wine. Esmerine didn't try to be polite and eat everything this time. She still didn't feel fully recovered from dinner.

The luncheon conversation was quickly doomed when one of the men brought up the Hauzdeen pamphlet. "Hauzdeen likes to blame the nobility for everything."

"You must not have read it very thoroughly," Alan said. She touched the tip of his wing, which was the only part of him easily within reach, but he didn't even seem to notice her attempt to divert him. "Hauzdeen actually takes the most balanced view I have found. He is quite sympathetic indeed to the fact that the treasury was depleted by the recent wars, which had just cause—well, *reasonably* just cause—"

"Of course it was just cause," Fiodor said. "They attacked the Lorrinese first—"

"But not entirely without precedent, certainly—the terms of the embargo—"

Dosia yawned pointedly. "You have to marry him, Esmerine," she whispered. "Think about having this kind of fun every holiday."

Before the argument could grow too heated, a few raindrops began to fall from the sky, quite unexpectedly, as it was still halfway sunny. They pattered on the canopy and moistened the grass, awakening the aroma of sweet greenery and the earthy smell of soil. This water smelled so different from the salty ocean.

"Look at that," said Ambra, pointing beyond her corner of the canopy. She sat at the opposite corner from Esmerine. "The clouds over there look cruel."

"Should we go inside?" Dosia glanced at Esmerine.

"Nonsense," Fiodor said. "All the food is laid out, and by the time we get everything packed away and inside, the storm will be over. Summer showers never last long, and we've got a roof over our heads." He called to the servants, "If it starts to rain hard, you can go take shelter in the shed until it passes."

"What is a shed?" Esmerine asked Dosia quietly. It didn't sound very nice.

The Ibronians laughed.

"It's a small outbuilding where some of the tools are kept," Fiodor said. "And a perfectly good question, no thanks to my rude friends." He elbowed the formerly drunk man—who seemed well on his way to becoming drunk again. They tussled a little, good-naturedly. There was talk of running races when the rain ended, and bets placed on who would win.

Up until then, it had been as ordinary a day as Esmerine could expect in such a strange place—a few pleasant moments with Alan, a few unpleasant moments with everyone else. A great sense of restlessness hovered in the air, as if something needed to happen, but she didn't understand what it was.

Then it seemed the universe was willing to oblige her. A hard gust of wind blew, almost tugging Ambra's bonnet off her head, disturbing hairstyles and lifting a corner of the blanket right into a bowl of berries. One of the servants rushed to correct it, but Fiodor said, "No, no, just hurry on into the shed."

The skies opened before any of the servants could make it, but they scattered off, clutching their hats. The rain was slanting in, and Octavia and Ambra shrieked and moved closer to the center, shuffling aside dishes of food. Falling water roared on the roof of the canopy and poured off the sides in sheets.

"Maybe we should have gone inside," Dosia said. "My goodness!"

Fiodor seemed to enjoy it. "It will be over soon, and in the meantime, none of you are made of paper!"

No, but Esmerine felt as if she were made of water, and her body wanted to join with the rain, even if it wasn't the water of home. Tickles and shivers ran down her arms and legs, and her head was full of the moist smell of it. Her toes convulsed, crying to be released from stocking and slippers. There was no way she would transform here, but the desire was so unbearable that she clutched her stomach and hunched forward, concentrating on the feel of her separate legs.

"Esmerine, are you all right?" Dosia asked quietly.

"Stomachache," Esmerine said.

"Chocolate is good for that," Octavia said, offering a tiny confection.

"No . . . thank you." Did Dosia not understand? Maybe because she had given up her belt right away she had never felt a burning need to transform.

Alan, on the other hand, had seen her desperation to transform when they landed on the island beach. He edged closer, and his eyes questioned hers. She shook her head a little. She didn't know what else to do but fight it off and wait for the rain to stop.

Everyone else was talking about how the sky looked and would it really pass soon and wasn't it all sort of exciting. Esmerine stayed hunched, battling with herself, panicked by how perilously close she was to losing control. She had worn legs almost continuously for two weeks, suppressing her true form, and now her nature was howling at her through the wind and rain to be set free.

Suddenly, the wind caught the canopy so sharply that it snapped free from two of its posts and fell on its side. Rain lashed Esmerine's face and arms. The pastries were instantly sodden. All the girls screamed and scrambled for their bonnets while trying to save the food. The men grabbed at the canopy, trying to sort it out. Alan stood and leaned down to help her up, but the wind caught his wings and knocked him a step backward.

Despite the chill rain now pattering on her skin, plastering layers of clothes against her, Esmerine's body was hot with the exertion of holding back. Panicked, she grabbed the edge of Alan's wing, a silent plea for him to help her, but before he could react, something inside her broke. She was going to transform and she couldn't stop herself. With one last great effort, she shoved back the impulse, scrambled to her feet, and tore off into the woods. Her knees quickly gave out. Her bones were already shifting. Transformation had never felt this intense— her legs were searing with so much pain that her lips trembled and a moan escaped her throat. She tore off her shoes, and before she had removed her stockings all the way, her legs melted together. The torn stockings dangled off the fins where once her feet had been. She yanked them free, tossed them aside, and collapsed.

Rain poured over her, pulling strands of limp hair across her eyes, trickling into her open mouth as she breathed hard with relief. In another moment, she became conscious of things poking her in places, and she pulled a few twigs out from under her. She pushed back her hair with shaky hands and managed to sit up and look back.

She was out of the way, but not entirely out of sight. Fiodor and one of the other men were looking at her, and Dosia was pointing and shouting something, but the rain obscured both voices and vision, and for a moment Esmerine felt she was in another world, looking out at them as if through a window or an enchanted looking glass.

Alan broke the spell, stepping into her world.

His wings were folded tightly around his body so the wind wouldn't catch them, but he had his left fingers curled around his eyes to protect them from the water running off his flattened hair. Esmerine recalled how her family feared being loomed over by him. She felt that way now, as he looked down at the fins that looked absurd spreading far beyond the hem of her dress.

He had seen her as a mermaid a thousand times as a child, and again when she visited her family, but in this human place, in these human clothes, she felt sudden shame. She tried to will her tail back into legs, but her body refused to obey so utterly that it was as if she'd forgotten how.

"Don't look at me!" she gasped. Then she twisted away, hands braced against the moist leaves carpeting the ground. Her arms, her dress, her hair, her tail—all were dirty now, covered with brown flecks of forest detritus and smudges.

He knelt beside her, folding a wing over her. "Esmerine."

"I don't know what happened . . . I—I just lost control. I had to transform. All the water—I've been a human too long. I couldn't stand it. And they all saw me, didn't they? I look so ridiculous—all wrong—I don't belong here!" She tried to look past him. "Are they still there? Tell them they can go. Tell them to *please* go."

"I told them I'd take care of you. They went to get out of the rain." He swallowed hard, looking her over, anguish in his eyes. When she had legs, they could both pretend, for a moment, that she might belong here. Not now. She had never been close to him like this, as her true self.

Her heart was pounding, and the rain roared in her ears. "You should go too."

"Why would I leave you alone in the rain?"

"I want to be alone," she said, but as soon as she said it, she knew she wanted the opposite. She turned around within his embrace, and slid a hand up to his collar, hooking her fingers around the soaked wool.

"I don't think you're being quite honest with me," he said.

Alan kissed her then, and she shut her eyes against the rain as he held her as a mermaid. In that moment, the hard decisions were gone. She felt that he saw her as a merman would—not disgusted or seduced—but as a real person. And he touched her as a merman would, letting her curl against him, lying in the grass, only with more wonder, and a hint of thrilling fear. They were both afraid of what this moment would mean; she could feel it in him.

It was one thing to kiss in the vineyard, in the middle of the night—inevitable that they would kiss that once, give in to a fleeting moment. This, though, was conscious, as if a new world had broken open. One of shared breath, of his fingers grazing her jaw and her ears, of her hands on his chest, feeling the lines of his rib cage and collarbone beneath his clothes, the solid realness of him—skin and bone and muscle.

"Esmerine—" he said, leaving it unfinished.

But what could he say? He couldn't follow her to the sea. She was the one who had to say something.

The sunlight moved in gently, and a heartbeat later the rain slowed but didn't stop. The light was a blinding white as the drops reflected the sun, and the rain warmed.

And then it stopped altogether, as quickly as it had started. Fiodor was right, it had been just a summer shower. The sun was golden again, the forest lush, like everything had woken from a dream. She briefly shut her eyes, clinging to the end of that moment in her life.

"Alan," she said. "I want to see what happens if I give you my belt."

Chapter Twenty-Three

Esmerine . . . I can't take it."

"I know you said you don't want it, but . . . that's why I trust you. I know you understand the weight of it." She clenched her hands. "You'll always know who I am, even if I give it up for the rest of this life. I mean, your mother was a mermaid, and you've never been able to go underwater, so I'll just be like you . . . and maybe I can still visit my family at the islands, and I can still write my book. I'll share everything I remember with you."

"I want you," he said. "Not an enchantment."

"But if I'm going to choose this life, I want to be able to move and dance in it—like Dosia. I don't want to be in pain. I don't want to . . . to transform like this."

He nodded, his expression grave. "All right. I'll accept it."

She lifted the hem of her skirt and gathered it upward, exposing the shining length of silvery scales, blushing as she did so. It was funny, she reflected, how she could spend a lifetime as a mermaid without clothes, but as soon as she put them on the mere act of removing them seemed indecent, even to reveal fins Alan had seen many times.

"Oh—it's trapped under these dratted stays."

He leaned forward to peer at her back. "I can see the links between the laces. Is anyone coming? Maybe I can free it."

"The servants are going to return from the shed at some point. Just hurry." She wanted it to be done. Would he act differently when he took the belt? Would her tail wrench back into legs?

Alan managed to hook the belt with a finger, draw the clasp around, and unlatch it. He tugged it, and it slithered from around her waist and fell away. She gasped, anticipating— something. She didn't feel any different.

Now they were both blushing quite thoroughly.

"That could have been planned better," he muttered.

"Something's wrong. I'm still a mermaid." She hesitated. "Do you feel any enchantment, holding it?"

His expression was serious. "It's warm. But not warm from your skin. Magic warm." He ran his fingers along the links. "And it sings."

"It sings?"

"Not with sound . . . It's like a vibration deep in my skull.

It's spellwork, I think. I just don't think it's working how it should. Tell me, if a siren gives a merman her belt, what happens?"

"Nothing. Unless she dies. Then her family can keep the belt and use its power."

"But what if she hasn't died?" Alan asked. "What if she just wanted to give it to him?"

"A siren wouldn't give her belt to a merman while she lives because she would need the power herself."

"But you've given me your belt. And I am the son of a mermaid. Even if I have the body of a Fandarsee, I must be a merman somewhere in my heart, because your belt doesn't enchant me."

"So even though I gave you my belt . . . its power is still mine? And my feet will still hurt." She wasn't sure whether to feel relief or sorrow.

"What if I give you something?" He put his fingers atop hers, guiding her hand to his collar.

Her fingers met something familiar—something tucked beneath his clothes, warmed by his skin. No—it was magic warm. The fine links of a siren's belt. She lifted the gold out into the light. As Esmerine rubbed the chain with her thumb, she heard a wisp of song, captured in the belt.

"Your mother's belt?" she breathed. She had never touched another siren's belt before. The day a mermaid entered training as a siren, her belt only left her waist once—during the siren's ceremony—until she died. And of course, Dosia and Esmerine were the first sirens in their family. Esmerine had never felt the magic of another mermaid, and she instantly knew what Alan meant, for she sensed it herself—a vibration deep within her, like the roar of the waves pounding within her heart.

"I needed stronger magic to be able to fly this long distance with you, so my father gave me my mother's belt," Alan said. "Your belt enhances my strength . . . maybe my mother's belt is the magic *you* need to become fully human on land and still be able to return to the sea."

"But we each started with a belt, and we'd each end with a belt. How is it different?" Esmerine hardly dared hope there really could be a way to be a part of the land and the sea . . .

"Yes, but there is a power in each of us *giving* one another something so precious, as opposed to merely having the siren's belts we each started with."

"You would really give me your mother's belt?"

"The greatest gift my mother could give me is the freedom for you to be a mermaid *and* a human."

Alan lifted the belt over his head, unfastened the clasp, and slipped it around her neck, looking straight at her with dear dark eyes. As the weight of the chain fell on her breastbone she felt a surge of power, the warm, bittersweet power of love that lasts through death and distance.

She placed her belt around his neck, tucking it beneath his collar where his mother's belt had been.

Now when she pushed the change, her tail obediently split. She trembled in Alan's grasp as her bones shifted, her scales melted away, and her fins curled into toes. She could tell right away that it was different this time. It didn't ache the same way. She could hear the faint song of the ocean inside her.

Her breath shuddered. She threw her arms around his neck. "Alan, I feel it. It's working."

"You're not even on your feet yet."

"But I know already." She was starting to cry, and then shiver, and she clutched his damp hair. She was still crying when she started to laugh.

"I want to see you walk!" he said, pulling her to her feet.

She knew the pain would be gone, but it was still shocking to feel nothing but her feet on the soft forest floor, no searing or aching or tickling, besides that her skin was sensitive without shoes. Hand in hand, Alan and Esmerine ran across the clearing, and for the first time in her life, she could keep pace with her oldest friend.

Chapter Twenty-Four

When they emerged from the woodland path, Dosia was framed by an open back door of the villa, her concern plain from her hesitant stance even before Esmerine could clearly see her face. Esmerine thought of limping forward and surprising her, but she was too excited to slow her steps or hide her smile. Dosia ran to meet her.

"What happened? My goodness, but you're both soaked!"

Esmerine threw her arms around her sister, almost too giddy to speak, so Alan had to tell much of the story. His version was very dry, but that was all right. She'd give Dosia the details later.

"I could teach you human dances!" Dosia said.

"Well . . ." Esmerine glanced at Alan. They hadn't talked over their future plans at all. "If I'm going to stay on the surface world, I should tell Mother and Father right away. I can visit you again soon, but they'll be very worried."

"That's true," Dosia said. "I'm just not ready for you to leave yet. But promise to visit again. And let me give you some money to take to them . . . they can exchange it with the traders and get proper window nets."

Alan nodded. "It's just three days from Sormesen to here. Maybe two, if flying together becomes easier. Of course, we should stay for dinner. No sense leaving until morning. So Esmerine can start her dancing lessons, if you like, just leave me out of it."

"Leave you out of it!" Esmerine protested.

"I don't care for dancing."

"Do you know how?"

"Well . . . Fandarsee don't dance."

"But mermaids do. Consider it research for our book."

Esmerine was by no means a natural at human dances, and yet it was so glorious to move freely, without any pain, that she felt almost as if she were flying. Human dances were understandably less fluid than mermaid dances, and seemed mostly a matter of memorization—keeping track of whose hand to take and which side to turn to and what foot to place where. Alan frowned his way through, possibly because they periodically had to link hands with other partners, and no girl seemed capable of touching his wing without giggling except Christina, who came with her own set of problems.

"Christina grabs me like she's about to arm wrestle," Alan muttered during a break, sipping his wine while tucking his right fingers beneath the collar of his vest, as if they could hide out there until the dancing ended.

Esmerine didn't enjoy swapping partners either; the drunk man had a very sweaty hand, and Fiodor was always talking, but she couldn't hear half of it over Octavia hammering the pianoforte.

It was all great fun, and yet Esmerine was anxious for the day to end. Worries began to drift through her mind—what would Alan's father say? Alan had sworn to return when their trip to the Diels ended. Could he forbid their relationship? And her family—her heart sank when she thought of explaining. How disappointed would the other sirens be?

"I'll be known for the rest of my life as that strange mermaid who ran off with a Fandarsee," she wailed to Dosia in the middle of the night. They should have been sleeping hours ago, but there was too much to talk about.

"Oh, darling, there are much, much worse things to be," said Dosia.

Chapter Twenty-Five

Once upon a time Esmerine had come to the island to play and had seen a boy on her beach. A boy with wings and a book tucked in his vest. A magical boy who made her heart ache, who made her young self understand what yearning meant.

Now her island was the place she would marry that boy.

Dosia loaned her own wedding dress of white striped silk with a white petticoat underneath, and beaded slippers. Esmerine sat on a rock while Dosia pinned her hair in complicated coils and pinned flowers in strategic places. She fastened a delicate necklace of blue and silver beads around her neck. "Don't look so worried," Dosia said. "You look absolutely lovely. Like a girl in a painting or a sonnet. I wish we had a mirror."

Esmerine shivered with anxiety. "It's not going to be a fine wedding by anyone's standards. At first Alan's father wasn't even going to attend unless we had it in the Floating City."

"What changed his mind?"

"Alan's little sister! She has a great talent when it comes to handling him. Alan and I have been working on a little writing together . . ." She hadn't intended to tell a soul about her book about mermaids until it was perfect. "And she told me to give him a copy of what I've written so far. Apparently he's only impressed with mermaids if they're sufficiently intellectual."

"Well, you should have no trouble with that."

"I suppose not. He never said a word about the writing, but he sent a letter giving Alan permission to marry." Esmerine toyed nervously with the beads at her throat. "Still, I'm not sure I'm glad he decided to come."

Dosia laughed. "I think it's marvelous. You'll have the most amazing stories to tell your children."

When they went to show Esmerine's dress to their mother, Octavia was talking with Esmerine's parents, who were sitting on the rocks, sampling wine for the first time, while Swift tried unsuccessfully to engage Tormy in conversation, and Belawyn was telling a frowning Christina that being an old maid really wasn't so bad. Alan's eyes alighted on her, and Fiodor thumped his arm with a jaunty fist.

"Bad luck seeing the bride before the wedding, you know!" Fiodor said.

Alan frowned. "Well, that makes no sense."

Esmerine felt very grown up with Alan beside her in his fine scarlet waistcoat and a hat with an owl feather, and all her family and friends admiring her wedding gown. Whenever her eyes swept over the water, dark heads ducked out of sight. Esmerine was sure she'd caught Lalia Tembel staring a few times.

Still, nothing made her feel less grown up than the arrival of Alan's father.

"You are certainly fortunate the weather is good for such a rustic ceremony," Alan's father said, surveying the scene. A few bare-breasted mermaids were draped on the nearby rocks, and the hem of Dosia's dress was wet from wading out to embrace them. The sky was blue, with only smudges of cloud, the water a darker reflection of the sky. She wondered if the beauty of the vast sea struck him somewhere deep inside, if he thought of Alan's mother.

"It's always good this time of year, Papa," Karinda said. She winked at Esmerine, then peered around. She was wearing a little fur capelet that Esmerine could tell was new from the way Karinda kept preening and straightening her collar. Merry looked fascinated.

"Hmm," Alan's father grunted.

Esmerine hadn't seen much of Alan's father since the day nearly four months ago when Alan brought her back to the Floating City to explain the situation. "I am not at all surprised," Alan's father said, before embarking on a tedious explanation of how much trouble they were in for, how he expected Alan to know better than that, how he had doubts that Esmerine would be able to properly assimilate.

"Esmerine already assimilated just fine at the bookstore," Alan had said. Esmerine moved into the apartment over the shop and Alan acquired a newfound appreciation for her "hoodwinking" until the debt to his father was paid off, while she learned the ins and outs of the shop and met a new nemesis in sums.

"You both look lovely," Alan's stepmother said, stepping forward to kiss their cheeks in turn. "And the setting may be rustic, but at least we're all here. Should we take a stroll before the ceremony begins? Do we have time?"

"A little." Alan's father checked his pocket watch. "Three o'clock, you said?"

"Yes," Alan said.

Alan's father took a packet of folded papers from his vest and gave it to Esmerine. "There you are."

As they walked off, Esmerine unfolded the paper. She couldn't imagine what it could be, but the words she had slaved over, that Alan had helped her polish again and again, leaped out immediately—now covered with black notes in Alan's father's tidy, slanted hand. She flipped through them—every page nearly smothered with corrections, crossed-out words, and notes.

"I didn't mean for him to critique it!" She was almost speechless, her throat tight with something between fury and embarrassment. Alan, however, made a funny laugh.

"Dear God," he said. "He must have loved it!"

"Loved it? There isn't a word in here he left alone!"

"To take the time to tear it to bits," Alan said, "I can tell you he loved it."

⚡

Merfolk were scattered across the rocks and the water. The sirens, whom Esmerine had worried wouldn't understand her decision, had perhaps understood best of all, for they felt the draw to the surface world in their own hearts. Her family, despite tears—some unnecessarily dramatic tears, at times— had been dear to Alan, and Esmerine could rest easier knowing the family's standing in the village would be forever improved by having two daughters become sirens, even lost ones.

She had never thought, in her wildest dreams, that everyone she loved could ever be in one place, even for this fleeting moment. The joy of it wrenched tears from her own eyes, even as she spoke a new oath, one she knew she would never break.

"Alan Dare. Esmerine Lorremen," said Lady Minnaray, who had donned legs and a plain white dress to lead the ceremony. "In the eyes of the gods of the sea and sky, and all present here to witness it, you are now husband and wife."

Alan bent to kiss her, and as she leaned close to him, she nudged off her shoes and let her bare toes tickle the moist sand.

Acknowledgments

The seed of this book began almost ten years ago. I'm sure I wasn't the only young writer who had the *Lord of the Rings* movie soundtrack on repeat and decided I needed to write a huge fantasy epic with war and tragic death and many points of view. One of the approximately forty plot threads in my attempt was the love story between a mermaid and a winged boy. (This is why you always keep your lousy older writings!) I resurrected the good part, but this time I wrote it with the soundtracks to Studio Ghibli movies in the background, which makes for quite a difference.

Since this is my second book, I'll try to keep it short. Thank you to:

Gordon Bell and the dearly departed Bernadine Bell, for crucial financial support of what must have seemed, at times, like a couple of artist bums.

Heather Cress, for being one of the first and only people to read this before I turned it in and for listening to me ramble as my life changed.

The Tenners, for the mutual support during our debut year; my critique partner, Jessica Spotswood; and all the rest of the writing community. I've got friends wherever I go; it's so cool.

Mickey Mercer, for telling what seemed like everyone she knew about my books.

As always, my wonderful family and friends; my editor, Melanie Cecka, who knows how to feed a girl when she comes to New York City; all the rest of the team at Bloomsbury for their hard work; and my agent, Jennifer Laughran, who makes me laugh and takes ridiculously good care of me.

My partner, Dade Bell, and his continued genius solutions to all my plot problems.

And, of course, all the fans. It's amazing how often the sweetest e-mails pop up on the worst days. I can't do it without you guys.